What the critics are saying...

"*Ms. Sparks* is a talented author who has penned a tale of love and dragons that I enjoyed greatly. I recommend this book to anyone who likes stories of dragons and shape shifters. *Dragons Law: Damon* is a keeper." ~ *Susan White Karen Find Out About New Books Coffee Time Romance*

"*Ms. Sparks*' world is definitely not more of the same old fairytale and legend retold. She has left herself with so many wonderful possibilities and avenues to explore in this new world that I hope she takes the readers on those journeys. Until her next offering, I will just jealously guard my copy of *Damon* and read it every time I feel the need for a shifter story." ~ *Keely Skillman, EcataRomance Reviews*

"*Dragon's Law: Damon* is the second of three stories she has so far in this series. One can only hope there may be more, but if not these are certain to have you wanting more as a reader. *Ms. Sparks* has been added to my list of must watch for Authors. If you would like sparks added to your reading, I recommend you give this series a try." ~ Tammy Adams

Dragon's Law
Damon

Alicia Sparks

ELLORA'S CAVE
ROMANTICA PUBLISHING

An Ellora's Cave Romantica Publication

www.ellorascave.com

Dragon's Law: Damon

ISBN # 1419952765
ALL RIGHTS RESERVED.
Dragon's Law: Damon Copyright© 2005 Alicia Sparks
Edited by: Briana St. James
Cover art by: Syneca

Electronic book Publication: April, 2005
Trade paperback Publication: October, 2005

Excerpt from *Ellora's Cavemen: Tales from the Temple II*
Copyright © Tielle St. Clare, Patrice Michelle, J.C. Wilder,
R. Casteel, Alicia Sparks, Angela Knight, 2004.

Excerpt from *Better Than Ice Cream*
Copyright © Alicia Sparks 2004

Warning:

The following material contains graphic sexual content meant for mature readers. *Damon* has been rated *E-rotic* by a minimum of three independent reviewers.

Ellora's Cave Publishing offers three levels of Romantica™ reading entertainment: S (S-ensuous), E (E-rotic), and X (X-treme).

S-*ensuous* love scenes are explicit and leave nothing to the imagination.

E-*rotic* love scenes are explicit, leave nothing to the imagination, and are high in volume per the overall word count. In addition, some E-rated titles might contain fantasy material that some readers find objectionable, such as bondage, submission, same sex encounters, forced seductions, etc. E-rated titles are the most graphic titles we carry; it is common, for instance, for an author to use words such as "fucking", "cock", "pussy", etc., within their work of literature.

X-*treme* titles differ from E-rated titles only in plot premise and storyline execution. Unlike E-rated titles, stories designated with the letter X tend to contain controversial subject matter not for the faint of heart.

Also by Alicia Sparks:

Better Than Ice Cream

Ellora's Cavemen: Tales From the Temple II anthology

Damon
Dragon's Law

Dedication

To Peter Steele, whose music is an eternal source of inspiration.

Chapter One

Damon scanned the decree before balling it in his fist and tossing it across the room. The nobility had spoken, and the successor to his father's throne would be named by the end of the month. Either he or Mace would be successful, the decision based upon which man married first. This went against everything his father stood for, everything Damon believed in. It went against the ancient laws of the land, yet the nobility who had ruled since his father's death were in need of a leader. And, as always, desperate times called for desperate measures.

His conflict with Mace was well-known, and if any of them thought that a marriage would end the schism, they were mistaken. All such an action would do would be to bring a new innocent into the mix, someone whose fate may be decided by forces beyond control.

Stalking to the window, images of his past flooded his mind. There was a time when marriage would have been a noble prospect. In fact, he had looked forward to it upon meeting his future bride. He had never met the Princess Kira until that night when he had taken her from her home, stealing into the night to capture her while she slept. It was the action of a thief, of a less than moral man, but it was something he felt compelled to do for more reasons than he could readily explain.

She had now been missing for six long years, and in that time his heart had died. He had fallen for her quickly and in doing so, vowed to not only marry her but to protect her from his brother. He had failed on both counts.

Mace had somehow gotten to Kira on the eve of their wedding night. His dragon fangs sank into her body, marking her for all who wished to see, making her his in a way Damon had not. Anger ripped through his body that night as he lashed out at Mace, vowing to kill him, vowing vengeance. In the confusion, Kira had disappeared.

Damon knew deep down inside that the woman—his woman—lived. Had she died that night, he would have felt an emptiness inside his soul. As it were, he felt a longing for her, a longing to have her in his arms, and a longing to find her. Only one man could grant his wish. He knew that somehow Mace had caused her disappearance, and now more than ever his need to find her grew fierce.

"What shall you do? Do you have a reply?"

Damon turned, having forgotten the -messenger in his moment of rage and self-pity. "I have a reply. You can tell them to make all the decrees they wish. My brother will never rule this land."

"But, sir…"

"No. You listen to me. You tell the counselors that I have spoken. I may be a bastard son, but I am the only hope this land has. Tell them they shall have their king by the end of the month, and he shall return with the promised queen, the heir of Karn."

"But, sir, Princess Kira is…"

"Missing. She is missing. And I vow to find her just as I vow to rule this land. You tell them that."

The boy nodded before ducking out of the room.

He would find Kira. There was no doubt in his mind. But to do so, he would have to face down his brother once more. Tomorrow night the eclipse would take place, and the sacrifice from Waydon would await the dragon who was victorious. Damon would go to the clearing and challenge Mace, and this time he would discover where Kira had been sent and how to get her back.

The oldest of his twin brothers, Kore, had aided him in his search for Kira, but nothing had been found. All they knew was that she had disappeared after he'd found her with Mace. That night, the vortex had opened, and Kore feared that Kira had been sent through it either of her own will or by force. Trader, the younger of the twins, agreed with his brother's assessment. As a scientist, he knew predicting the vortex was damned near impossible. It seemed to be outside of the realm of science and ruled only by magic.

But Damon loved Kira so much. He would fight science and magic to return her. Even now, even after the betrayal that bit into his heart, the image of seeing her with Mace cutting through his system, he knew there was an explanation. Mace must have forced his way into her chamber, must have convinced her to lower her blouse. That or he used brute force. Either way, Kira could not have gone to him willingly. She had not even willingly come to Damon the night he had stolen her from her home.

He closed his eyes and remembered a time when everything seemed possible. Another decree had been handed down from the nobility and the king of Karn. But he had been unwilling to marry a stranger and had taken matters into his own hands.

* * * * *

He had stolen into her room as a dragon, slipping in with the night. One strike from his tail had secured her state of sleep, but he knew that when she awoke she would be furious with him. At first. Then, as soon as the balm made its way fully into her system, her need for him would be so strong she would be unable to resist him.

Her sleeping frame enticed him so, he wanted to reach out and touch her lips with his fingertips, to lower his mouth to hers, but he resisted. Gathering her into his arms, he pulled her close and set out into the darkness in search of his hideout, a cave not far from the castle, but far enough to keep her safe from his brother and the nobles.

He watched her and tended the fire while he waited for her to awaken. Her long, red hair flowed down her back and hung off one side of the bed. Her lips were parted, plump, teasing him as she lay on her back, her soft skin tormenting him from across the room.

Finally, she stirred.

"You are awake."

"Yes." The word barely escaped between her lips, and her hands immediately went to her head. "Where am I?"

"You are safe." He moved to stand by her side and steadied her as she tried to sit.

"Who are you? Am I dreaming? My head aches."

"Shh. You are safe, and no, you are not dreaming. You are my prisoner."

She looked up at him, confusion clouding her face. "Your what?"

"Prisoner. I have taken you from your home, Princess Kira. You are fully awake."

"Get your hands off of me." She pushed away from him but she was still too unsteady to be successful. His hands grasped her shoulders again, preventing her from falling over backward.

"I mean you no harm," he attempted to soften his voice but had difficulty softening the raspy tone.

"Then why did you kidnap me?"

"You and I have much to discuss—when your head feels clearer. I mean you no harm. You must believe me."

"Release me now and I'll allow you to live. My father will have your head."

"Your father will not lay a hand on me. Do you know who I am?"

Her teeth captured her bottom lip, making it difficult for him to focus on anything save for those plump delicacies. "No, and I do not wish to know you."

"Ah, but I know you, Princess. And I wish to know you even better."

Her breath was warm against his face as her chest heaved. He knew he was playing a wicked game, one he had no right to, and the look of fear in her eyes coupled with a slight hint of curiosity fed his ruse. "And how is it that you know me?" Her eyes narrowed in challenge. He had hoped his future wife would be filled with fire, and she apparently was.

"Because you are the princess destined to marry a foreign ruler. Everyone knows this."

"I shall marry no one." She defiantly raised her chin, challenging him with the look in her eyes.

"But your father sees differently."

She waved away the comment, apparently unconcerned about her father's wishes. "What happened to my head?"

"You fell."

"When you kidnapped me?"

"Yes. " The word made its way out through clenched teeth. Kidnapping her was necessary, but that still didn't make it an easier to take.

"I'm not your princess. You have taken the wrong woman."

"Ah, but you are a princess, and you shall become a dragon Slayer." He stood, leaving her to contemplate his words as he turned to the fire.

"You are insane."

"We shall see tonight."

"No. We will not."

"You have fire in your heart. I like that."

"What do you want from me?" Hands on hips, she challenged him again as he bit back a smile.

"Come, sit with me. I will not hurt you, you have my word."

"I don't trust you."

"No, but you will. Tell me, what do you know of your future husband?"

"What concern is he to you? Are you his enemy?" There was a flash of hope in her eyes, which made Damon's stomach sink at the notion that she would befriend his enemy.

"If I say I am will you look upon me with more kindness or will you continue to scowl at me?"

"I do not scowl."

"You are now. Perhaps I bring out the worst in you. Now, about your husband…"

"He's a ruler. Or he's supposed to be. He and his brother have fought for years. Why am I telling you this?"

"Come sit by the fire and warm yourself. You are, after all, in your nightgown."

It was as if she had only noticed it now. A blush crept up her cheeks and her bravado was lost. She let out a frustrated sigh before joining him, but she was obviously careful not to sit too close.

He watched out of the corner of his eye as she pulled her knees to her chest and covered herself completely with her gown. Swallowing a smile, he turned to her. "Tell me more about your husband."

"I am not marrying him so there is no reason to discuss him. Why do you want to know?"

"I shall not reveal my secrets. Let us say you are of value to me."

"Do you plan to ransom me? He doesn't even know me, so I doubt you'll get a nice price."

"I have no plans for ransom. And I am sure any man will pay greatly for you."

He watched as she swallowed a lump in her throat. "Do you plan to kill me or send me away?"

"No. I told you. You can trust me, Princess. I have need of you, it is true. What I said before stands. You shall help me slay a dragon."

"Where are we?"

"My home. The dragon's lair."

Her eyes widened. "You are its keeper?"

"Aye, I am the dragon's keeper."

"Am I to be his meal?"

He nodded. "Yes, Princess. You are to be his meal."

"What good am I to you if it kills me?" she challenged, again lighting a fire beneath him with her strong will.

"He does not wish to kill you. He wishes to mate with you."

"I won't become a dragon's mate."

"You already are. As we sit here and speak. You and I may exchange simple words, but our bodies are readying for one another. You know it as easily as I. Your body is growing wet, your muscles are tightening. You feel a sensation here." He pressed his hand against her fur covering. She let out a tiny whimper as he stroked her through her gown. "A sensation you can't describe. You moan for me. You want to feel me inside of you."

Her eyes met his in challenge. "No. You imagine things."

"I will not take you by force. But you and I shall mate."

Her warmth called out to him from beneath her nightgown. Even though her eyes were wide, she made no move to remove his hand. This was the dragon's balm at work in her system, and he knew it was wrong to trick her this way.

"I will not mate with you or a dragon or anyone."

"You say that in disgust. What if your prince were a dragon?"

"I have no prince."

"Your marriage bond says differently."

"I am not a princess."

"Yes, Kira, you are. You are King Rudolf's oldest daughter. And I am a dragon. Your prince is a dragon, and you shall learn all there is to know about our kind before the next moon phase."

* * * * *

Kira tossed and turned in her big, iron bed. The dreams refused to let her rest. They came nightly, teasing her with a past she could not recall in her waking hours. It had been this way for the past six years, since she'd appeared out of nowhere in the middle of New Orleans. No one knew how long she had been in New Orleans or where she came from. The only thing she knew was that she woke up in a hospital bed after a week's stay, a huge, throbbing gash in her shoulder, a strange man by her side.

He wasn't the man from her dreams, the one who came nightly, claiming to be her lover, reminding her of a past she couldn't recall. While she was asleep, she saw his face clearly but the image blurred as soon as the sun rose. Need drove her forward as she made her way through the daytime in order to meet with him at night. He took her to another land, another time, another existence that she needed desperately to get back to.

He was the reason for the video games she designed. He was the reason for the emptiness inside her heart. Tonight, the dream was the same as always. They were in a cave, somewhere that appeared to be out of another time and space. Somewhere that reminded her of a home she had never been to.

* * * * *

"Where are you taking me?" she asked, unable to see in the endless blackness. But it wasn't endless. It only appeared that way from the other room. As her eyes adjusted to the dark, she could see a tiny sliver of light in the distance.

"I am taking you to bathe." He pulled her along with him, his hand wrapped firmly around her wrist.

A bath. She knew it was preparation for what was to come next. She wanted to protest, wanted to force him to take her roughly, wanted to be made to fight and scream. Anything to make him seem less appealing. But the truth was, she wanted his hot hands on her, and her desire for him was something that defied all logic.

Her thighs were already wet with her own juices. He had been correct when he said her body was preparing for him. It had started the second she awoke to see him stoking the fire, and it continued now as he pulled her behind him. She stumbled in the darkness and landed against his body, causing an instant reaction.

When he finally slowed his pace, she caught her breath and took in the spectacle that lay before her. The darkened room held nothing more than a deep, dark pool of water that would have looked inviting had it not been for the closeness of his rock-hard body and the anticipation of what she knew was to come next. She steadied her breathing, forcing herself to regain control. Her instincts were all but lost as she eyed the pool helplessly.

Her gut protested what her body wanted to do. The battle within her was something she had never experienced before and something she could not contain. She inhaled, watching the slow motion of the water and preparing herself for the mating that she knew she could not avoid. Her hands fisted at her sides, but her pounding heart reminded her that she wanted his body, wanted him inside her.

He inhaled sharply, the sound causing her to flinch. Fire shot from his mouth, taking her aback. Within seconds, the entire room was lit with candles of all shapes and sizes, each casting a somewhat romantic glow over the pool of water that seemed to dance with invitation.

It called to her, promising her wonders she had never before known, vowing that once she entered she would never be the same. The dragon would have her body, but he would also have a piece of her soul. Even as her brain protested, her feet ached to move forward.

"Wait." He held her back when her muscles tensed in an attempt to enter the water. "Let me warm it for you."

Fire shot from his mouth just before the water bubbled then settled. Once more, he turned his snarl upon her. His gray eyes didn't seem so harsh, his hand still gently lay against her arm. He released her and motioned for her to move forward. She obeyed, wanting more than anything to feel the release the pool and the man promised.

Kira stepped into the warm water, swearing that nothing had ever felt so heavenly. She hadn't been aware of how her muscles ached until she sank into the pool. Closing her eyes to the sensation, she opened them when she felt him enter the pool behind her, his presence signaled by the rippling of water around her body.

"Sit," he ordered.

She obeyed, sitting on one of the raised steps in the pool. It reminded her of the baths she had read of long ago, the kinds that existed in tales she no longer believed.

Taking it in from this perspective, it didn't resemble a pond or an indoor lake. Instead, it looked more like a grand mosaic tile tub. And her keeper looked like a king.

He put his hands in her hair, pulling it around to her back. "Lean back," he whispered against her ear, his warm breath sending a shiver of longing all the way to her core. She lay against him, reveling in the feel of his body pressed firmly against hers. He poured warm water over her head, moving gently as if he knew he was stoking a fire deep inside her. The sweet scent of soap rose up, lulling her into a calmness she never thought she'd feel with a man such as him. As his hands moved in her hair, she let out a moan.

His fingers worked at the knots and tangles, gently fingering through them. When he was done, he pulled her head back into the water to rinse her hair. She moaned again as the water slid through her hair, dripping into her face. Warmth filled her, removing any inhibitions she may have otherwise felt. It was as if she couldn't control her body. Her vision blurred and her senses heightened when confronted by the incredible man who moved to stand in front of her, a clear bottle in one hand.

She watched as he dripped liquid from the bottle into his other hand and then formed lather with it. He moved closer to her, reaching out to touch her breasts, which were already anticipating his touch. Now the desire to have him choked her, leaving her helpless and vulnerable.

Her nipples hardened and puckered, begging for more than a gentle touch. Begging to be teased, tormented, bruised. She arched her back and moaned as he took his time, gently wiping the lather onto one breast and then the other. Lifting them, caressing them. Ever so gently.

She clung to his shoulders for fear of falling backward if she did not. He moved his hands to her neck, massaging there before sliding down to her shoulders and her back. Her breasts ached for his touch to return. He blew a soft breath onto them, one that made her skin tingle and sent a wicked sensation all the way through her body, igniting the flames inside her, caressing her like a lover would. And she knew he would soon be her lover. The gentle dragon would take her and make her his.

"Lie back."

She leaned against the second step, feeling the hard edge press into her back. His hand moved down to her stomach, sending a trail of desire as he touched her, spending an eternity caressing the skin there.

She moaned, begging him to touch her *there*. He didn't. Instead, his hands moved down her legs, caressing them, lavishing the soap onto them. He raised them out of the water to steady them against his shoulders as he sank beneath the surface. His hands moved up and down the length of her legs while he breathed a constant stream of warmth against her skin. His hands then moved to her feet. Slowly. First one, then the other. Concentrating first on the heels and then the toes and then the ankles.

She closed her eyes, unsure of what to do with her hands. Her body refused to move for her, refused to do anything save yield to his touch. His roughened hands, the ones she knew possessed the power to kill, moved as if they were made of silk. And her longing to have them roam over every part of her body was more powerful than anything she'd ever felt. He finally released her, moving her legs back into the water, then rose above her, the water dripping off his hair making the dark mass look as if it were covered with crystals. His silver eyes caught the candlelight, reflecting his desire for her, a desire she felt, too.

He moved away from her. Only a step, but she suddenly felt cold having been abandoned by his touch. She watched as he took the bottle and placed it into her hand, his fingers brushing against hers. "Wash me," he commanded.

"But you're not through with me," she protested, her desire for him overriding her senses.

"No," he warned, "I'm not through with you."

She followed his lead, taking his hair into her hands first. She worked the soap through the thick mass of black tangles and was amazed at how the tangles became soft waves when she rinsed it. What was left behind was a thick swirl of ebony hair that teased against her nipples as she worked. A vision of the hair falling into her face assaulted her with such ferocity she almost slipped into the pool. She clung to him to right herself. He moved his shoulders, unaware of his effect on her, encouraging her to wash him there.

She moved her soap-covered hands along his shoulders, tracing the scars down his back. Then she turned him so he faced her and began rubbing the soap into his chest, paying attention to the same sensitive areas he had so gently washed, trying not to think about the hardened muscles of his body, the slick skin she wanted to feel pressed against hers. Her care was rewarded with a smile that made his face look incredibly inviting.

When she moved to take his penis into her hands, he pushed her hands away. "Not yet."

She bit her lip, wondering if he would become her lover tonight. Surely that was what he had planned when he brought her here. And she was more than willing to oblige. Her senses were spinning with intense longing to have him, to hold him, to be one with him. Still, he resisted her touch.

He lifted her, placing her on the ledge surrounding the pool. The cool surface sent a chill through her heated flesh. The heat from his breath sent a wave of desire through her. "Spread your legs for me."

She obeyed. Nothing inside her wanted to protest.

"I want you to lie back," he gently guided her with his hand, only letting go when her head made contact with the surface. "Are you ready for me?" he asked.

"Yes," the word was barely a whisper. She quaked and quivered, aching for him to touch her, the desire coming from a place she couldn't understand.

"You're so small. If you're not ready for me, I could split you open." He traced a finger along her inner thigh, careful not to touch the one place she longed to be touched.

"Then do it."

"No. First you must prove you are ready for me." His words teased against her skin.

"How?" Her brow wrinkled. She was more than ready for him—so wet she couldn't stand it. She was on the edge and all her nerve endings were tingling.

"Take this," he pushed the soap bottle into her hand.

"What do you want from me?"

"I want you to show me where you want me. How you want me to take you."

Her hand gripped the glass bottle. He wanted her to slip it inside her, wanted to stand there, face-to-face with her inner core and watch her, wanted her to move the bottle in and out the way he would move in and out of her. All this, she knew without words. "I can't," she protested.

He placed his hands on either side of her and pulled his body out of the pool. Holding himself up, he pushed his cock against her. She swallowed hard. Never had she felt anything like this. He pressed against her, willing her back to arch, bringing her closer to him. "If you want my cock inside of you, you will do as I tell you." His words held a warning, a threat. They excited her as she gripped the bottle.

Her hand shook as she looked into his gray eyes and moved the bottle toward her lower half. She had never touched herself before. Never had the desire to do so. He slid back into the pool, his breath *there*, warming her skin as the cold bottle moved down her body.

"You're doing very good, Slayer. You make me wonder how it will feel to be inside you, to join with you. You want that, right?" She nodded, unable to speak. The tone of his voice was both commanding and heated. Moving her hand, she parted her lips. She had never felt anything so incredible as her fingers moving against her skin. Closing her eyes to the sensation, she recalled how it felt when her maids removed the hair. They teased her skin and rubbed her lips in a way she could never explain. And they did something to some other part of her. *This part.*

Her fingers closed over her swollen clit as she gasped for breath. She looked into the dragon's eyes, reveling in the silver glow of his approval. She was pleasing to him, a thought that made her only want to explore further. Continuing to stroke herself, she stared into his eyes, watching his reaction. She wanted him to touch this part of her that throbbed with longing. She began rubbing there, Moving her fingers in tiny circles. She refused to tear her eyes from his even as the waves of ecstasy approached. A moan escaped her lips as she slid the bottle into her opening, slowly but steadily, bringing a pleasant smile to the dragon's lips.

Her lips were stretching, stretching beyond what they did when she placed her fingers inside her body. She arched against the bottle, moving it further in, taking all of its slender width into her body.

"You're so deep," he crooned above her. "Have you ever had anything so big in your pussy?"

"N-no," she managed.

"Has anyone ever touched you before?"

She bit her lip and nodded.

"Ah, yes. Tell me who. Tell me who touched you, Kira."

"You. In my dreams."

She hadn't realized she had spoken the words until his face lit up with confusion. "You dream of me?"

She nodded. "I think I'm dreaming now."

"Tell me what I did to you." He stilled her hand, holding the bottle deep inside her, stopping the movement. "Tell me and I'll let you play."

"You touched me," she began. "Please," she begged. The pressure of him holding the tapered bottle there was too much, as it filled her so completely, stretched her beyond her imaginings. The desire to have it move was so intense she was on the verge of begging when he slid it out, allowing only the narrow tip to stay inside her body.

Images of him loving her in another time and place assaulted her at once.

"Tell me." He slipped the bottle back in gently, as if he were aware that the slow movement was torture.

"You liked to touch me. *Here*." She rubbed her clit as he moved the bottle in and out. He moved it slowly to the very tip and then pushed it back into her all in one motion. She moaned each time it went out, cried out each time it filled her. Oh, to have him there! Moving with her, pleasuring her the way he was doing now, only with his body.

"What else, Kira?"

"You liked to lick me."

"Like this?" He bent, replacing her finger with his tongue, giving her clit a short lick.

"Y-yes. Like that." Her voice wasn't her own now. It was filled with longing, with desire. She couldn't control her body as he moved the bottle and then slipped it back into place. She began to quiver, to shake, and was afraid she would break the glass, her movements were so fierce.

"There's a good girl. Come for me."

He moved the bottle even faster, grazing against her skin as he slid it in and out. She heard the sound of her juices squeezing out against the glass. The slapping of flesh against flesh only heightened the sensation of what he was doing to her body. "What else did I do to you?"

"Your fingers. You put your fingers inside of me."

"Mmmm. Like this?" He slid a finger in with the bottle, stretching her even further.

"It never felt like this."

"No, it didn't." He slid his finger out and pressed it to her lips. "Did I ever let you taste yourself?"

"No." She took his finger into her mouth, shocked at how the movement thrilled her. She sucked at it, delighting in her own taste. Too soon, he removed it. "Please."

"Please what? You want some more?" She nodded. "Then tell me more about what I did to you, about what you dreamed."

"I don't know," she protested. Gods, she wanted him inside her. She wanted him to slide into her like the bottle was, to fill her completely and make her quiver, to hear his skin slapping against her like the bottle was doing now. The quivering started again. This time she clung to him, her fingers in his hair as he moved the bottle in and out, in and out.

"That's it, my sweet. Come for me. I'm so big, I'll hurt you if you're not ready for me." His voice was gentle, but the words only ignited the fire even further.

He pulled the bottle from her pussy. She moaned when she heard it release from her body. "No," she protested.

"I'm going to give you something much better," he promised.

An alarm sounded before she could take him into her body. Shit. Reality came crashing down around her, and the man who had become a regular fixture in her dreams once more disappeared into nothingness. She couldn't even remember his name when she was awake. Only in her dreams did he become real. Well, there and in her video game. But he wasn't a real flesh and blood man.

And if he were somehow a part of her past he obviously didn't miss her enough to come looking for her.

In the past six years, no one had showed up on her doorstep looking for a lost lover.

She rolled over in her bed and looked at the clock. Today was the day. She would catch her flight to New Orleans in a few hours and by tonight she would be another person entirely. Tonight, she would be the ultra-popular video game creator whose past didn't matter to the masses of fans whose ravenous desire for the new game pushed her six months ahead of schedule. Tonight, she would be confident, poised, composed. She hoped. But most importantly, she would find a man in New Orleans who vaguely looked like the guy from her dreams. And she would try to overcome the longing inside her chest.

Chapter Two

Kira smoothed down the blue velvet fabric of her dress, enjoying way the softness lingered against her fingertips. She didn't look half bad, she decided, giving herself a close once-over in the hotel's full-length mirror. Her hips were a little wider than she would prefer, her breasts a little more on the verge of spilling out of her gown, but overall, not bad.

It had taken three weeks to choose the right dress for tonight's festivities. She had gone through several goth numbers heavy on the black lace and satin ties, but this one with its princess neckline and nipped waist seemed to be exactly what she needed to boost her morale. And it was working. For the first time in six years she didn't feel like she had "freak" stamped on her forehead. For once, she felt as if she had an identity, something to cling to in a world of harsh reality. But it was all a smoke and mirrors act. She knew that beneath the confident external layer rested the heart of a woman whose life was still filled with too many unknowns about her past to even begin to plan a future. All she had was right now, this moment.

Her lines were well-rehearsed. If anyone asked anything about her life she had a fairy-tale background she could recite with very little effort. She hoped. And not a single word of it had anything to do with ending up in a hospital bed and not really knowing who she was.

The only thing she had remembered when she woke up six years before, in the hospital bed, was a name.

Damon. Who he was or how he fit into her life she wasn't sure. She remembered him calling her Kira so she adopted the name, finding peace with it even if it had been born from a feverish dream. She still hadn't recovered from whatever had happened to her. Every now and then she felt it in her system, some presence that shouldn't be there. When it became too much for her she secluded herself and disappeared into her imagined world.

She hadn't realized how much her time with Leland had scarred her. She bore his mark just as completely as she bore the mark of whatever it was that had left its imprint on her shoulder and its DNA in her system. Leland was certain it was a werewolf, but Kira wasn't so sure. The hunger that overtook her had nothing to do with blood. She fed on sex, or at least, she would have had she been able to give into the craving that started somewhere deep within her body and radiated out through her pores.

That was the reason she pushed men away. Leland included. The need was so strong, so primal, she knew if she unleashed it, it would devour her. And she had nothing to offer a man except for what looked back at her in the mirror. Her past would remain a mystery, just as it had since she woke up in the hospital, the feeling of fire shooting through her body.

"Freak" didn't begin to cover who she was or what she was, and until she understood the changes raging inside her she could never trust herself. Sometimes she felt as if there were a beast living within her, lying in wait. Maybe Leland was right. Maybe the genes he couldn't identify were those of a werewolf. It was as good an explanation as any. Lately, though, her handle on reality seemed a bit more concrete.

She had labored over her video game with the obsessive energy of a woman possessed by demons. The world, the characters, the conflict—they all seemed to fill a void within her, helping to squelch the rising flames of insanity. The man who had become the hero, whose face seemed so real and familiar, had been her savior at a time when very little was certain.

And as she worked the throbbing ache in her shoulder seemed to die down to a low hum, always there but no longer threatening to destroy her. It had taken two years to create the first *Dragon's Law* game, and now it was the hottest video game in the country. The second of the series was almost complete and tonight the cover and plot would be revealed to the rabid audience downstairs. That was the reason she had ended her seclusion and come to New Orleans.

Secretly, she had also hoped it would be a way to reclaim her life—or start a new one. Item one on the list was to find a man who didn't care about her past and wasn't interested in a future.

Taking in a deep breath, she memorized her surroundings, reveling in her first adventure on her own. The room was impressive—from the large jacuzzi tub to the sheer ivory drapes to the bed that was so obviously not made for one person. The four posts hinted at all kinds of wicked games that could be played if only she had a willing partner. This was the Princess Suite and tonight she would rule the convention with all the grace of Diana and all the dry wit of *Xena, Warrior Princess*. And she would finally find someone to have a wild, hot, no-regrets fling with—no matter what.

There was one last item missing, the one thing that would complete her wardrobe. The necklace had seemed to come out of nowhere. She swore that she'd looked on the table at the antique vendor's booth at least three times before finally spotting the necklace whose large blue stone called out to her. The man sold it to her for a hundred dollars. She had clutched it to her breast like a rare prize as she happily handed over the cash. It had to be worth more than that, but the vendor had seemed more than satisfied and Kira didn't dare to ask any questions.

The charm had immediately calmed her nerves, assuring her that this trip to the South was exactly what she needed in order to build a life for herself. This would be her metamorphosis from girl-with-no-past to woman-who-controls-her-own-destiny.

Running her fingers along the large blue stone, she felt the jolt of electricity that went through her body every time she had touched it these past two weeks. She still hadn't placed it around her neck for fear that the energy would seep into her skin and consume her with its power. Tonight, she would take that chance. Her dress was made for this necklace, and it looked an awful lot like the one the princess sought in her girl-power video game. It would be her charm, her security, and her courage. Every time she felt unsure, she would run her fingers along the gold chain and down to the sapphire and draw strength from the gem.

And every time she touched it, somewhere deep inside, the longing for home crept upon her, surprising her with its intensity. The feeling was always fleeting and always replaced with a calm certainty that she was almost there.

Inhaling slowly and then letting her breath swirl around at the back of her throat before exhaling, Kira lifted the necklace from its velvet bed. Her fingers came to life, feeling as if ten thousand needles were pricking them. *He is almost here*, a voice inside her head promised. Yeah, right. No fairy tales, no happy endings. Not tonight. She just wanted to have sex, to feel skin on skin, to know how it felt to touch and be touched without feeling like a science experiment.

Every time she had been naked with Leland his eyes lingered to her shoulder and the mark that defied his comprehension. As a scientist, Leland was obsessed with the unknown, but he seemed even more drawn to the unknowable. She realized finally that he viewed her as the link between himself and a world of mystery. And, God, how she hated him for that!

No one would ever see the bite mark again. The clear outline of two rows of large, inhuman teeth capped off by deep puncture wounds of two sets of fangs, upper and lower, had been cleverly disguised by a tattoo artist in Memphis. The rose vine that draped across her shoulder and snaked around to the back of her neck hid the mark to anyone who would have seen her bare shoulder. Only two people knew it was there, and one of them wouldn't ever see her again.

As she laid the necklace against her skin the sensation that swept through her didn't stop at her fingers. Her heart leaped in anticipation. The steady rhythm it had held before, bum-bum, bum-bum, was replaced by a quick bum-bum-bum as the sapphire rested against her, filling her with a renewed intensity she couldn't quite explain. The gold chain hummed against her skin, sending an unidentifiable wave of energy through her body, making her recall for a second dreams she had tried to forget and a man she had never known.

"You're being silly," she told the reflection in the mirror. "He doesn't exist. He can't exist."

Dragons were not real. Not in this world anyway. In the world she had created, well, that was another story. Her fascination at times seemed to move beyond mere curiosity. And the necklace only added to her mysterious background, as she was certain she had seen it before.

Slipping her room keycard into her boot, she gave herself one last glance before reaching for the doorknob. Her stomach turned at the thought of going downstairs and walking into a room with three thousand people she didn't know. Oh, she had talked to some of them online, but she had never met them face-to-face, and Kira was not one to go out on her own—ever. Things were different now. She was all she had, and if she was going to go somewhere, it sure as hell was going to be alone.

"Here goes nothing."

Turning the doorknob was probably the most difficult thing she'd ever done, but once she stepped into the dimly lit hallway, she knew she was doing the right thing. Her entire future awaited her downstairs, as tonight would be her first night to speak in front of a crowd about her game. It would also be the unveiling of the latest video game cover. Her stomach churned at the thought of having her work on display in such a manner, but she reminded herself that this was who she was now. In the past three years she had transformed herself from Leland's science project to Kira, Warrior Princess. And she had every intention of defending that title tonight.

The elevator opened its mouth to welcome her inside. Thank God it was empty. If there was one thing she hated more than walking into a room full of strangers, it was walking into an elevator full of them. Besides, she still needed a minute to calm herself down enough to walk into that main convention room. She almost wished she had taken her agent up on her offer to accompany her. But no, Kira had insisted on coming alone, on trying to prove something to herself. It had seemed like a good idea at the time, but right now it seemed ridiculously childish.

Her hand strayed to the necklace and the familiar comfort swept over her, reminding her of what she'd overcome, of who she was and of who she wanted to be tonight. There was no mistaking the *who she wanted to be* part. She wanted to be the kind of woman who could meet a strange, gorgeous man at a sci-fi convention, bring him up to her Princess Suite and fuck the hell out of him for the weekend. Something deep inside her told her that she wasn't quite that woman yet. But by the end of the weekend, who knew?

* * * * *

There were two things on Damon's mind as he stalked across the ballroom, parting the crowd with his massive frame. First, he had to find the woman he had defied space and time to track down. Then he had to secure the amulet that he knew had made its way here. Figuring out how to get back home followed a close third, but for now he would focus on the first two. Lifting his nose in the air, he could smell the earthy scent of his home and could sense the dirt from Tyr-LaRoche as only a man born there could. Whoever possessed the amulet had brought it here to this strange land that he had little desire to spend another second in. But the amulet, the only proof of his birthright was here somewhere, and he knew that when he found it, he would find Kira. Something in his gut insisted on it.

As Kardoth's son, he had a right to the throne and fully intended to present his case to the council at the next meeting, something he knew Mace wished to prevent. With Kira by his side and the amulet safely around his neck, he would be able to accomplish this. His brother had done a wonderful job in hiding the amulet far from the reaches of the nobles, but he hadn't counted on Damon's determination when he threw the charm through the portal and into the deep abyss. The look on his face when Damon had jumped in after it was priceless, making him almost wish he could have had someone immortalize that look in stone. In the days since he had been on this planet, he had come to realize that Kira was here as well. Her life energy called out to him, making him imagine her breath in his ear with every step he took.

Mace had taken everything from him, and he swore he would gain it all back. Hatred had consumed him at first, when Mace's trickery had cost him Kira, but now that he knew the truth and knew that she was somewhere on this planet, he was determined to find her and put an end to this battle between himself and his brother. Sill, her betrayal burned inside him. "It's not what you think." Her words echoed in his head. How could it have been anything more or anything less than what he had witnessed? Their love had been secret, sacred to him. He knew he would never love another, but tonight love mattered not. Tonight, need drove him forward and vengeance and lust battled for control. He would find Kira, whether or not she wished to be found, and he would return her home.

This strange planet held many wonders, but none of them had interested him for more than a passing glance until tonight. He had felt her when he entered this land they called *New Orleans*. The dragon inside him had raised his head and snarled, sending a flash of heat through his body, as soon as he came within a mile of the woman—his woman. He had spent the better part of the day tracking her to this *hotel*. These people, primitive as they were, had an advanced language, one that was similar to those known throughout the universe, though their spelling and pronunciation were strange to him. He wondered only briefly if they had perhaps descended from one of the tribes that had left his home planet thousands of years prior. His reflections were quickly shaken from his mind when Kira's life essence had called out to him, sending pulses of energy through him, beckoning him to move within the walls of the hotel and seek out its hiding place.

Strange costumes adorned the various humans who were gathered in the large, grand room. They looked nothing like the clothing worn by those out on the streets. These were more like things he read about in books, from the fairy wings to the long, flowing gowns. His long, black robe did not appear to be an oddity among the men here, many of whom wore similarly styled cloaks.

The music that surrounded him was also otherworldly, sounding nothing like the peaceful rhythms of his homeland. The crush of the bodies weaving in and out of the center of the room was enough to leave one's head spinning with wonder. All the while, he focused on the energy swirling around him, energy from home that sent fingers of heat through him, gently guiding him forward, seeming to come from the left and then from the right. It was enough to drive a common man insane, but Damon was too focused for insanity, even though his insides churned with anticipation.

He had waited this long to claim his birthright as ruler of Tyr and would not allow the opportunity to slip by because his brother had forced the fates' hands by sending his bride through a portal to another world. Their father's death had left the land in a state of turmoil, the council torn between electing Kardoth's legitimate son or choosing the one who carried Kardoth's full curse, the one born out of wedlock. They forced his hand with their new decree, and now he was here, millions of miles from home, seeking out the one woman who owned his soul.

Damon sometimes cursed his birth as the oldest child of Tyr's former ruler. Had Kardoth married Silla, Damon's life would have been much different than it turned out with Kardoth marrying Lyrra first. Mace's mother had announced her pregnancy and forced Kardoth's hand. And now Mace and Damon's rivalry had reached its height.

They had fought bitterly, when the moons eclipsed one another, when he should have had the upper hand. Again, the fates had interfered and in the last seconds Mace's hand had closed over the necklace that hung from Damon's neck and flung it into the night before he collapsed to the ground. It was then that he whispered the words Damon longed to hear. "She is in there." Damon stared into the darkness for mere seconds before he had made the decision to leap first and think second, and that was what had led him here.

His fingers pulsed with the memory of the stone and the way it felt beneath them. It warmed to him, sensing the beast deep inside, sensing the power it held over his destiny. Some said the spirits of the ancients lived in that stone, guiding those who sought it, controlling those whose monsters raged and threatened to destroy them. On

Tyr, controlling one's demons was a necessity—and it was all but impossible for Damon without the two things he needed most, his amulet and sex. For some on Tyr sex was enough, but for others, like Damon and his father, the amulet, forged long ago, was necessary.

It was no coincidence that Damon's ability to control the dragon and the proof of his birthright existed in the same stone. Mace had known that and had sought to destroy him with the knowledge. But now, as his heart raced, pounding inside his chest, he knew he was close to recovering it and Kira and returning to Tyr to reclaim that which Mace vowed to take from him.

The crowd parted just as Damon's skin began to burn, alerting him that he was growing closer. He closed his eyes, attempting to quell the beast inside, something that was increasingly difficult without the amulet. The beast raged for a second before resting its head, waiting, warning Damon that *he* was growing weaker while it grew stronger. If he did not recover the amulet soon he would no longer be able to control the beastly urges and all would be aware of the secret he kept closely guarded. He felt the dragon's talons pierce his flesh from the inside, warning that it would be unleashed soon if he did not find a willing mate. And tonight, the only mate he sought was the one Mace had taken from him.

Regaining control, he looked up as the doors to the ballroom opened and *she* stepped through them. He knew her instantly even though his mind and heart contradicted one another. Kira *was* here, on this tiny planet. Swallowing the lump in his throat, he shook the images of his lover from his head before looking at the woman again. On second look, she was not the woman from his past, even though her face had the same shape he had once traced lovingly with his fingertips. No, she lacked the fire and intensity of his lover. But every inch of him pounded with the thought that Kira was in this room with him.

Mace, again, had the upper hand. He had known Damon would leap into nothingness to find the woman he had lost, and now, both Mace and the universe at large were playing a cruel trick on him. The woman looked so much like Kira, but beyond her looks, there was nothing in her demeanor that spoke to him.

The woman was of average height, nothing spectacular to look at save for the glow radiating from her skin and the softly rounded hips that swayed as she practically glided through the doors in her high black boots and short blue gown. She stopped just short of fully entering the room as Damon observed the fiery luster of her hair, a red unlike any he had ever seen before. It wasn't the blood red of his brother's hair, but more like an autumn sunset back home, when the sun began dipping its head low and the moons started their ascent. It, too, wasn't spectacular, he thought, as his fingers longed to reach out and grab a handful of it, weaving their way through the heavy mass.

No. Nothing special at all about her. He insisted this was so even as his heart pounded at the very sight of her slightly upturned lips and the way her eyes darted back and forth as if she were mustering up some kind of false courage before taking another step forward. But the woman exuded courage, even if it was not the kind of firebrand bravery his Kira possessed. No, hers was subtler, the strength-in-reserve type that only surfaced when all other wells had run dry, just as his mouth suddenly had.

If her eyes locked onto his any tighter, he would feel them squeezing into his system. Even from here, he could see the green flecked with blue and could practically feel the pain exuded from them, a warning to him and any other man who might seek her attentions that she was beyond having.

His amulet pulsed, calling out to him from between her breasts, forcing his attention to the rise and fall of her skin as his eyes broke their embrace with hers and focused on the object he had recently lost. The dragon licked at the back of his mind, warning him that if he did not regain his strength soon, he would lose control, something he did not wish to do. Still, the beast teased, warning him that he grew weaker every second he sought to defy the curse upon his kind.

No normal human would know that the man standing dumbfounded by the beauty who still had not fully entered the room was not at his full strength. He moved on legs much longer, much stronger than those of the other men and walked with a kind of barbarian grace that spoke of his years as a warrior. But he was growing weaker by the second, unsure of how many true days had passed since he and his charm had parted ways. It had been bad enough to lose Kira, but to find her double standing here, wearing his amulet was enough to send him over the edge.

Time was not on his side as his patience faltered. The woman stepped across the threshold, her eyes avoiding the area where he stood, and he knew he must act quickly. Too much was at stake to waste time wondering about such nonsense as how a woman's curves would fit into his embrace and whether or not her nether hair held the same fiery glow as the mass of curls that flowed down her back.

He had a kingdom to save, a title to claim and a brother to defeat. There was no time for soft skin, green eyes or other promises he could never fulfill. Even if he knew he would need her in order to survive this night. She was not his Kira, he reminded himself, but she would make a lovely substitute.

The need threatened to overtake him, humming in his ear, whispering warnings, sending the blood from his brain to his cock. He tried to curb it by closing his eyes and imagining the real reason he was here, visualizing his victory. The monster inside would have none of his rationalization. What it wanted tonight was what was tucked between the woman's shapely thighs, and it wanted this with a need that threatened to take Damon's sanity.

He fisted his fingers, drawing all the energy he could summon, hoping to quell the urges that were suddenly upon him. Her scent permeated his brain, even though he stood across the room from her. The magick inside the amulet was stronger than both of them and possessed the ability to send him her fragrance as well as the silky feel of her hands on his back.

She licked her lips, and a shiver went down his back as he practically felt them whisper down his spine from across the room. Her nails would rake against his back as she dragged her hands across his flesh. He could sink himself into her, claim her as his if only he could coerce his legs into moving across the room, parting the crowd and taking her.

This was a civilized world. This was not a land of dragons and might. A man would risk much if he moved with such haste, and Damon could not afford to alert these strangers to his real intent, his real identity.

Still, the need for her throbbed between his thighs, causing the blood to pulse in his cock as he once again swore he could feel her behind him, her breath on the back of his neck, hot, ready, crying out for the kind of release only he could give her.

Before the night was done, he would know how it felt to sink his hands into her lush hair and to taste her lips. This he vowed as he began stalking his prey, his eyes on her body as it softly swayed and moved through the crowd uneasily.

* * * * *

For the fiftieth time that night, Kira's heart threatened to beat right out of her chest. If she didn't know any better, she would think someone had played an awful trick on her. How could anyone outside of her company know what the new video game cover looked like? Someone had to have leaked the information because the man standing across the room from her, the man who seemed to be heading her way, was dressed exactly as her hero was on the new cover. He towered over most of the men in the crowd, and his shoulders were wider than her hips! If a Greek god could lend his body to a mere mortal, this man would have it.

He was massive, well over six feet tall, and was built like a romance novel cover model. And heaven help her if the slight pout on his lips didn't jar her for a second, sending her to another place and time. Maybe she had known him before. He was certainly eyeing her with interest, making her wonder if she had once been the kind of woman who could attract a man like him. His long, dark hair hung to his waist and was twisted in various braids. The square set of his jaw warned that if his full lips ever smiled, she would lose her heart, and his gray eyes were so intense she could practically feel them sweeping across her as the rest of the room faded away into nothing.

Her breath hung in her throat as she watched his corded muscles move beneath the fabric of his black robes. There was little to the imagination as both his large chest and his ample crotch were on display for everyone to see. All one had to do was let the eyes wander south, and the mysteries of the man would be more than evident beneath his tight leather pants.

Throbbing need flashed through her body at the thought. Ever since she had stepped into the room it felt as if her hormones were in overdrive. Her fingers dug tiny half-moons into her palms as she tried to still her ragged breath, which seemed to rage even further out of control as she watched his long, muscular legs glide across the room, moving him closer and closer with every step he took. Her tongue darted out of her mouth, wetting her lips as anticipation crawled up her back. God, to have her hands on him! *This* was what she needed this weekend. *He* was what she needed. A man who could fulfill the kinds of fantasies the men in her video game only hinted at.

And he looked so much like her hero. A neatly trimmed beard covered his chin, making his mouth appear to be a forbidden sensual treat. She licked her lips just thinking about how it would feel to run her tongue along his upper lip and feel the hair tickling her skin. She could only imagine what it would do to other, more sensitive parts of her body, parts which had only been touched by the man who came to her in her dreams.

The mysterious mouth was not the end of his appeal. His deep gray eyes spoke volumes to her from across the room. He was a man with a past, probably with more baggage than she had, something she didn't really need.

But he also looked as if he had a dangerous edge, like there was some wild man living inside the civilized—okay, partially civilized—demeanor. Dressed like an ancient magician but looking more like a warrior, he had to be one of those romance cover models. Those guys often frequented these events, seeking work as video game character models. If that was the case, then this guy was so far out of her league she couldn't even see home plate.

Nobody like that would ever want the formerly frumpy Kira. She grabbed the edges of the blue stone that hung around her neck, mustering up false courage. He would want Kira, Video Game Goddess. She could rule this convention with an iron fist if she wanted, her game being one of the most successful in the past year. If only she could pull herself out of her shell long enough to find the man and say, "Hey, baby, you wanna go up to my room and screw my brains out?"

Okay, even Kira, Warrior Princess, wouldn't come up with that line. No, she would just watch him all night, wondering how it would feel to be wrapped in his strong arms, to feel those sensual lips close in on hers, to feel his body sliding against hers in the heat of passion. Then she would go back up to her room and use the glass dildo Mariah had given her as a "going-away present" last week. "Just in case," the petite blonde had shrugged when Kira opened the present. Yeah, if ever there was a just in case, he was Mr. Greek God. Yum-my!

But she knew deep down inside that she wasn't ready for a wild weekend, and as his eyes stayed locked on hers, she felt like a deer caught in the headlights of a runaway train. And she knew she had to do something to get away.

"Kira Montgomery!" Saved.

Kira turned slowly, unsure if she could break the gaze with Mr. Video Game God. His eyes burned into her back, sending out a warning she couldn't readily miss as an unfamiliar voice echoed in her head. *You're mine.* "Constance, how are you?"

Even as Kira wrapped her arms around her former co-worker, she felt the eyes on her, but she was more than thankful for the reprieve.

"I'm great. How are you? Famous video game designer now, I see."

Constance looked exactly as she had five years ago when Kira had still been on the road to recovery and was only beginning to play around with computer animation, much to Leland's dismay. Five-foot-ten and gorgeous. She was the kind of girl guys walked across the room for. Until tonight, no one had ever crossed the room for her, no one except the man who still kept a close watch over her even though his approach had come to a halt.

"Not so famous."

"Come on, everyone here is buzzing about your game and the unveiling of the new cover. Tell me, did you really have a gorgeous cover model to pose for you?"

If only. She had never seen the guy before except in her dreams. And her rendition of him was sadly lacking when the real thing stood just a few yards away from her.

"No, there was no model."

"Well, come on to the bar with me. We have to catch up. I design for Starr Games now."

Constance had always been more of a star than a video game designer, so the occupation seemed to fit. She even wore a pair of tight leather pants with her lace-up corset, something Kira wouldn't dream of trying to squeeze into.

"Okay, sure." Anything to get away from those eyes that still threatened to cut right into her and made her body throb with longing from across the room. She swore she could smell him on her, could almost stick out her tongue and lick the air, tasting his fragrance there, nothing but man and sweat and lust—the three things she needed most in her life.

She tried to concentrate on Constance's voice, listening to the words, but not really focusing on their meanings. Something to do with her job and how much she loved it. Kira hated being inattentive but the man had not yet given up. His pursuit had only changed intensity as he followed them to the bar, staying several steps behind, trying to blend in. As if. That was like trying to hide an elephant behind a two-by-four. It wasn't likely to happen any time soon.

As she slid into the booth in the hotel's bar, Kira winced at the cold leather against her backside. Whatever had made her wear a thong? She should have known her dress was bound to ride up at some point in the night, leaving her exposed. But the chill sent a delicious wave of desire through her as she imagined the man's tongue running along her already swollen clit. Never before had she been this ready for sex. She just knew that if she stood up she would leave a puddle of longing on the bench as proof.

"What'll it be?" the waiter asked as he approached.

"I'll take a whiskey sour," Constance said, smiling at the young man who, Kira was sure, was cute enough. Somehow he didn't hold a candle to the man who had claimed a seat at the bar.

"I'll have a glass of champagne."

"Sure thing."

"I'll be right back," Constance announced before sliding out of the booth. Kira watched her walk away before her eyes again locked onto the gray eyes of the stranger, who was once again heading her way.

Bringing out the brassy, bold Kira that she had practiced in the mirror was going to be more difficult than she imagined. Especially now that she had a target in mind. She would give anything to have the nerve to be the kind of woman to pick up a stranger, have wild sex with him and never ask his name. Why was it that some women could and some could only dream about it? She owed it to herself to have a fling, right? As he approached, she tried to force the words out, "Hey, baby…" They never made it, though.

"Fancy seeing you here."

The man stepped dead in his tracks as Leland eased forward, coming from out of nowhere. Kira watched the stranger's hands grip into tight fists as his veins bulged his irritation. He took a step backward, blending into the shadows as Leland slid into the booth.

"Leland," she tried to hide her disgust but failed.

"You look great, babe."

"What are you doing here?" She tried to compose herself, to keep her voice under control, but it was damned difficult with the man of her dreams lurking somewhere in the darkened bar while the only past she had ever known sat across from her, a smirk plastered on his lips.

"I caught the red-eye. We have to talk. I think you're in danger."

"What else is new? I'm always in danger, according to you."

He ran a hand through his wavy blond hair. He had never worn it this long before, and his eyes bespoke hours spent at the computer, probably analyzing her DNA again. Usually, he was a handsome enough guy, but tonight the stress of his obsession was clear on his face. "Can we go somewhere to talk?"

"Not now. I'm with a friend."

"Constance. I saw. It won't take long."

"Later. She's coming back in a few minutes."

"It can't wait long, Kira. Here's my cell number." He scribbled on a napkin and then pushed it toward her. "We have to talk tonight. It's urgent."

He slid out of the booth as she folded the napkin. With Leland, everything was urgent. He had been seeking proof of werewolves his whole life. Every time her blood changed, he freaked out. He hadn't had a sample in a while and was probably needing his fix just to see what her chromosomes were up to. Between his obsession and his damned computer program that was designed to predict changes in her DNA, it was enough to drive her crazy.

But, no, fate had to send in the icing on the crazy cake. The waiter returned just as the man moved from the shadows to slide into the booth, taking Leland's place.

"Can I get you something, sir?" He placed the drinks in front of Kira as he turned to the stranger.

"That will not be necessary." The thick accent that rolled off his tongue reminded her of Dracula's Transylvanian accent, but wasn't quite as sharp. Tiny chills crept up her back and she flushed beneath his gaze, wishing she were anywhere but there.

"Let me know if you need anything else." This was directed at Kira, but she couldn't find her voice to answer before he turned on his heels and headed back to the bar.

Don't leave me here with him, Kira wanted to scream, but the words died in her throat along with every ounce of courage she possessed. Whoever he was, he was intent upon looking straight into her tonight, something that left her more uncomfortable than she could have ever imagined, even as the heat coursed through her body, warning her that desire often knows no bounds.

Chapter Three

Kira reached for her champagne, hoping the bubbly liquid would calm her nerves. Nothing was likely to help, as his steel gray eyes seemed to look right through her and go straight to her core. She held the glass to her lips, hoping he would speak soon so she wouldn't have to, hoping the champagne wouldn't end up a mass of bubbles in her stomach, hoping he'd stop looking at her as if he wanted to eat her alive.

"I am Damon," he said finally.

She wished his introduction would have had a calming effect. No such luck. Instead, the sound of his name vibrated through her, leaving her all but gasping for breath at the intensity of the invasion. Flashes of memory came to her but none of it made sense. *Damon.* She should know him. Something inside her screamed out recognition while the rest was just a haze. This is just a coincidence, she silently convinced herself. So he had the same name that had been the only connection to her past that she possessed. It was a common name, wasn't it?

"I'm Kira." Safe conversation. Stick to names, occupations, not *come to my room, please*. Thank God he made no attempt to shake hands. If he had, she wasn't sure she would have been able to do it without turning into a puddle of mush.

"Kira." The name fell off his lips as if it were an endearment, and something about the sound of his voice was making her hotter than she'd ever been before.

There was something chemical going on that she couldn't quite explain. Nearness to a man had never caused her to lose control of her desire in such a way. Her body practically throbbed with longing just looking at the man sitting across from her. It took every ounce of strength she had not to reach out and touch him to see if he was real.

"Yes. I design video games." Still a safe topic.

"Video games?" He wrinkled his brow, obviously disapproving of her chosen field.

"Yes. Let me guess, you're a model." She reached for the champagne again, almost ending up with a lapful of it when the glass teetered beneath her fingertips. She blushed at her clumsiness but recovered quickly enough.

"A model?" All he did was repeat what she said. And he did it in a way that made her body hum with desire. He had only said five or six words to her, but she had already decided that he was the one she wanted to have the wild fling with.

Her eyes strayed to his massive hands. His long, thick fingers made her wonder what they could do to her body. She had a vivid picture of her spread against her hotel bed, legs open, waiting for him to nestle himself between them and drive them both toward ecstasy.

He caught her staring, and she tore her eyes away, but not before an image of him naked made its way into her mind. God, she would give anything to have his hands on her body. Her pussy clenched at the thought of having those long fingers stroke her inner thighs, run along her sides and tangle in her hair. She was staring again. She really needed to stop that.

"So, what do you do?"

"Do?"

God, did the man not know English? He was beautiful, but the way he kept repeating and staring was doing nothing for her self-esteem right now. Why *was* he here, at her table, when he could be anywhere else? And why did she want to reach out and touch him as if she knew him? She was staring, she knew. And that knowledge caused her to flush all the way down to her chest.

"Yes, what do you do? Are you from New Orleans? What brings you to the convention?" She fired off one question after another, hoping to find some steel inside them, hoping to find something to calm her nerves because the champagne sure as hell wasn't doing the trick.

"I am from Tyr-LaRoche, and I am here to reclaim something that is mine."

Now, why were his eyes locked onto her chest as he said the words? God, if he wasn't a model, he needed to be because one look from him was enough to make her want to buy anything he attempted to sell. But there was more to him than surface good looks. There was a sadness in his eyes, a hint of betrayal as he glared at her, making her feel as if she were the source of his misery.

"Have you found it?" she managed, well aware that her breathing had become labored just being near him.

"Yes, I have found it. It is…"

"I'm back." Constance had either the best or worst timing in the world.

Damon straightened when she returned. Kira's back stiffened, hoping the cute blonde wouldn't slide in next to the man she wanted to claim as hers for the weekend.

"Constance, this is…"

He stood, towering over them both. "Damon."

"Well, Damon, it sure is nice to meet you." Constance didn't get a handshake either.

"It is nice to meet you." He gave her a slight bow before turning back to Kira. "You and I shall finish this later." There were ten thousand messages hidden in his voice, and every one of them felt like an intimate caress. She watched, dumbstruck, as he left the bar.

"Who was that?" Constance whispered, her eyes following him to the door.

"I have no idea."

"Wow. You don't run across one of those too often. Must be a model."

"Must be."

* * * * *

Her name was Kira, a fact he had not overlooked. The princess he had stolen, the woman who was his, rightfully his, shared that name. That was not the only similarity. Everything about her, from the way her hand rested on her champagne glass to the way her eyes delved into his soul reminded him of the woman he had known. Looking into her green eyes, it was as if his Kira were in there, somewhere, lost. She needed him as much as he needed her. He was certain of this fact. More importantly, she wore his amulet, which was something that he could not overlook. She belonged to him, and he had every intention of reclaiming her tonight.

Two hours later, Damon's eyes followed her as she stood before the room, stammering, obviously aware of his attention to her. He made her nervous, uncomfortable, and he excited her. This he could feel from across the room, as if the amulet around her neck were sending her biorhythms to him, making him painfully aware of her inability to concentrate on anything but him.

Never had he known anyone outside of his family to possess the amulet. None had worn it save for himself and his ancestors. There was no way of knowing what it would do to her, but one thing was certain. The absence of the charm combined with the inability to reach out and touch the woman who now possessed it was going to cause him to lose his sanity if he did not recover it soon.

As she spoke, he imagined her face merging with his Kira's, the woman who had taken his heart as a casualty of the war between himself and Mace. They were there on his bed, her shoulder bared, Mace's mark on her flesh. Damon had stumbled backward, the betrayal a physical blow. Rage had overtaken him as the dragon leapt from its reins to lash out at her. Its intention, he had known, was to kill her but Mace had interfered. She had died that day, whether in reality or only in his mind, he wasn't sure, and had never been seen again.

But now, he needed the gods' help to remove her image from this woman's face. If this Kira had known him she could have revealed his true face, ruined his chances of returning home. Yet she seemed intrigued by him and completely unaware of who he was—and what he was.

Yet, she had the amulet and the spell of protection that went with it.

His ancestors had been unable to control their demons, unable to squelch the dragons inside themselves, until the amulet had been forged from stones deep within the bowels of the planet. It gave power to those who possessed it. It had been given to him by his father as a means of control until Mace ripped the amulet from his neck and tossed it into the vortex.

Now, the woman's fingers closed over the necklace as she turned to the side, the room filling with applause as she moved to the side of the stage… Behind her, on a large projection screen, an image came to life. It was then that his heart literally stopped beating.

Whispers and excited awe filled the room as those standing near him turned to gaze at the man whose face looked down upon the crowd. He could read the writing scrawled across the picture. *Dragon's Law: The Quest.* The dragon hummed in his ear as his heartbeat began a wild rhythm. How had the woman known his face? How could she see into his soul, announce him to the world for what he was?

Mace was a master manipulator, but could he have commanded her performance? As her eyes locked with his, his lover's face became clear once more, and the pain she had inflicted on him came rushing forth as the dragon threatened to take control. The blood rushed into his ears as he awaited the crowd's response.

No one seemed surprised. She bit her bottom lip and sent him a helpless gaze as the roar of the crowd intensified and the applause heightened. The necklace pulsed around her neck, forcing her heartbeat into Damon's system, causing their hearts to beat in time with one another, forcing him to look at her, not that he could tear his eyes away now if he wanted to do so.

Then she spoke again. Legends of men and dragons, a foreign planet where dragons ruled and men fought for dominance. The land could be his homeland, but the woman should know nothing about Tyr. Then the word spilled from her lips. A game. This was all a game, some elaborate device meant for entertainment. These humans took it as such, but he understood even further. She was toying with him, mocking his pain. Worse, she was mocking his need to reclaim his title. This was an elaborate game set into play by Mace. Only Mace did not realize how Damon intended to win.

Questions poured in from all sides, yet he was intent upon reaching the platform where she stood. Just as he approached, determined to take her into his arms and force the secrets from her, crush her against him until he could not feel anymore, a man stepped between him and the crowd that consumed her, pulling her beyond his sight.

The man's jaw was set in clear determination as his lips pressed together. "Who are you and why are you following her?"

Damon looked down at the man, who was much taller than most of the men he had encountered on this planet. Still, he was no match for a man whose insides housed a beast. "Get out of my way," he growled.

"No. I don't know who you are, but she's mine. Understand? Stay away from her."

The declaration of property sent a jolt through him and his own possessive nature rose to the occasion. He would not allow a simple Earth man to claim the woman he intended to have as his own. "Move aside." The man did not budge and Damon attempted to move around him in order to go after Kira.

"Wait one minute. I want to know who you are." The man's hand closed around Damon's biceps with a grip he had not expected from such a man. His physical size did not match the strength of his grip or the fierce look of a predator that radiated from his eyes.

"No one touches me." The snarl that escaped his lips, combined with his bared teeth, showed more of his nature than he would have liked. The dragon threatened to emerge as it sensed the challenge of another beast that had been pushed too far.

"Shit." The man removed his hand and took a step backward as the word escaped his lips. It was a human curse Damon had heard numerous times in the past days. "How do you know Kira?" The challenge in his eyes waned as he now looked at Damon with outright curiosity.

"We just met."

"I'm Leland. Excuse my overprotective instinct. Kira and I are…close."

"You said she was your woman."

"Perhaps I …exaggerated."

The sudden change in the man's demeanor had him more on alert than he had been when the man's hand had touched his flesh. "I have no time for this."

"Neither do I. That's why I'm here. I need to warn Kira. She's in danger."

The dragon inside him whispered a warning, but it was one he was already well aware of. If there was a danger to Kira, he knew the source. "I sense no danger." He practiced the words before uttering them to ensure his ability to speak them clearly. The only thing he felt since making the connection between Kira and this woman was an overwhelming sense of danger. And he was the cause.

"Well, I do. And I know that there is more to you than it appears. I know what lurks inside you, and I'm here to help."

Damon stopped cold and stared at the man. How could he possibly know what lived beneath his skin? Kira. There was no doubt in his mind now that she and his lover were one and the same. Only his Kira would know his secrets and only she could have shared them with her lover, which this man clearly had been, even if he was no longer. "You know nothing of me."

"I know there's a change that overtakes you, one that you can't control, one that lingers just beneath your skin, threatening your sanity."

"And what makes you think you know this?"

"I pay attention. Let me introduce myself. I am Dr. Leland Tambourne. I study creatures that aren't supposed to exist. For fifteen years, I have been tracking a creature that changes by the moon. And I think tonight I've found him."

"Let us not talk here. There are too many around." The man nodded his agreement before leading Damon through the crowd that was still blissfully unaware that the man moving among them had the ability to kill.

The moon of Earth was dim compared to those of his homeland. Yet, as they stepped out into the darkness, Damon felt a familiar tranquility washing over him, making him almost imagine that he were in his home, stepping out onto his veranda. If he closed his eyes he could imagine her still lying in his bed, fresh from their lovemaking, exhausted yet wanting more.

"She bears your mark," the man said after they had retreated into the cover of night.

"Who? Kira?"

"Yes. You know her, then?"

"Knew her. Once."

"She doesn't remember her past. Nothing before six years ago. I found her after you left her for dead."

"I did no such deed." Yet deep inside, he knew that he may have left her for dead. Rage had blinded him and the dragon had been out of control. There was no way of knowing what he had done to the woman he had once loved. The one thing he knew for sure was that he had not sent her here.

"The bite mark on her shoulder. It is yours?"

He swallowed hard. No, it wasn't his. It belonged to his brother. Mace had given her the balm that would make her more than human but less than a cursed dragon. Piercing her skin with his fangs had been enough to place his poison in her system, changing her forever. Taking her away from him. Whatever else had taken place between them did not matter. Mace had marked her as his, and Damon could not touch her. "I have not touched her." The lie tasted bitter on his tongue as he denied their past and their love—just as she had.

"Then there are more out there? More like you and me?"

Damon turned his attention from the night sky to face the man who could not possibly be a dragon. Yet his strength was more than human. "I don't know what you mean."

"I'm talking about werewolves. Man by day, wolf by night when the moon changes. Come on, man, level with me. Are you a werewolf?"

Wolf? The creature he had seen in the zoo, howling at the moon, raging quietly over its captivity? Damon had felt a connection to the animal and its position as a prisoner in a world where it didn't belong.

"I am not a wolf. "

"But your mouth—when you snarled earlier, it showed the change. I saw your teeth, the perfect outline of what I have studied on Kira's shoulder for six years. She is the key between the two of us, between us and whatever created us. Her body is changing and she is going to need our help."

He heard the words but did not have the ability to comprehend them. Every second that passed seemed to bring a new revelation, yet they all ended with the same conclusion. His Kira was alive, and her betrayal continued to live inside him like a virus attaching itself to him.

"I can't help you. I want nothing to do with her."

"But you were following her. Stalking her. You looked at her like a predator looks at his prey. If you don't want her, then what are you doing?"

He would not trust this man who claimed to be a wolf. He had not been on Earth long, but he had never encountered another creature on any of the worlds he had visited who was cursed to change by the moon as he was. Until now. The connection did not require trust or understanding. It only required warning to stay out of one another's paths.

"I have no interest in her," he repeated his vow, yet it felt empty.

"Then leave her to me. She is going to change soon, and she will need someone who understands."

"How do you know this?"

"I have tracked her DNA for six years. I know the changes her body is undergoing. The change is slow with some, quick with others. The bite that was inflicted upon her was not deep enough to cause immediate changes. It took time."

"Are you certain it was a wolf?"

"A wolf, or whatever you are. Which would be?"

"A man. Nothing more than a man."

"I don't buy that, but you can tell yourself that all you want. I know there's more to you than that. I've studied creatures that don't exist almost half my life. I know you are not human."

The man's questions ended when Damon's refusal to answer became apparent. He had no desire to share his curse with Kira's lover, and he had no idea if he could trust the man's assertion that Kira did not remember him. Part of him wanted to walk away from this New Orleans and find his way home. But there was still the matter of the amulet, and the fact that he could not return home. Then there was Kira, the woman who he would not leave without.

His planet was in danger, though. His people were at the mercy of his brother and his enemies, who would have him declared a false leader without the protection of the amulet. Only Kardoth's son, his firstborn, would be able to wear the amulet. Only his first son would be cursed as Damon was.

All the men on Tyr shared the curse, but Damon's was part of the original line. The firstborn male son in the original line would need more than sex to quell the beast inside him. He would need the ancient stone of Tarnu, the one residing in the amulet around Kira's lovely neck. Mace

had known Damon's weakness, had feared his challenge
for the throne, and had taken the eclipse as an opportunity
to rid himself of Damon's presence.

But there were more problems that just those. Damon
had no idea how to get home. The vortex that had opened
that night had brought him here, to find Kira, to follow the
amulet, but now that window was closed and there may
not be another avenue of return. Everything inside him
knew Kira held the key to his salvation. He just wasn't
sure if he wished to reopen the old wound. But he was
inexplicably drawn to her. He needed her now just as he
had needed her years before on his home planet. Then,
even as he swore to protect her, he had been unable to
resist her, unable to stop touching her.

He had spent the day watching people watch her,
watching them play this game she had created and
wander through the world she had drawn so perfectly, so
beautifully. None of them knew this world actually existed
somewhere in the stars they looked upon each night. None
of them knew that the only reason he was here was
because he and Kira were connected to one another.

Worse yet, none of them knew the secret beast
lingering just beneath the surface, threatening at any
moment to break free and mate with the first available
female. If he did not mate soon, he would lose control in a
way that he could not explain. It was only with those of
Kardoth's line, the firstborn sons descended from Rylan,
the original dragon of Tyr.

The dragon hissed in his ear, warning him that
tonight he may not have a choice, and if he continued to
grow weaker, if the fever continued to spread through his
body, he may be forced to choose a mate and risk

remaining on this planet forever, not that he had much choice in the matter right now.

But Kira... Her face loomed above him, calling out to him like his salvation. He knew she held more in her hands than just his charm, she held his future. Taking a mask from one of the display tables, he slid it over his face and made his way to the masquerade ballroom.

He would be gentle and suave. He would force the dragon to submit to him as he romanced the woman who called out to him in his dreams. But in the end, he would take her tonight. The sun could not set on him once more without mating. To do so would unleash the dragon. And to deny himself her sweet flesh once more was unthinkable.

* * * * *

Kira barely made it to her room before the fever overtook her. The heat was so intense it was difficult to breathe. She wanted to rip the blue dress from her body and step into the flow of a cold shower. In her momentary attempt to regain control, her hand brushed against the necklace that lay on her chest. The cool stone soothed her inner ache with a warning that the relief was only temporary. Soon she would have to find a man.

The bite on her shoulder throbbed a warning, too, and she felt as if someone else were living inside her head, urging her to go find the stranger she had met earlier. Everything inside her screamed that he held the answers to her past. And it wasn't because he was so incredibly beautiful. It was because somewhere deep inside she knew he was the cause of this, even if nothing seemed to make sense anymore.

She felt as if she were a stranger inside her body, which was not entirely untrue. But she couldn't go back downstairs, not with Leland lurking about, threatening to drive her back to that dark place she could not escape. Life as a lab project was not for her. No more needles, no more tests to see what was going to happen to her reproductive organs or her blood or anything else. All she wanted now, all she needed, was Damon, the one who looked so much like the man whose face had driven her to create an alternate world. The man who, she knew, had come to her in her dreams, and who was now here for her.

The masquerade. As she caught sight of her fairy wings hanging in the hotel closet, she remembered that the masquerade was starting downstairs. She had been so distracted, first by Damon and then by Leland, that she had forgotten the remainder of the night's activities. The masquerade was the perfect place to become someone else and live out her fantasy. She changed clothes, determined to find some self-confidence in her costume.

Self-doubt crept up her back like a poisonous snake as Kira contemplated what she was about to do. Everything inside her wanted to invite Damon into her room, damn the consequences, and make him hers for the weekend. She deserved it, after all. But there was something so intense about his eyes, something that made her yearn for more than just a weekend with the hunk. Deep down, she knew what it was but she wanted to deny that fate had anything to do with what was going on inside her head.

She knew him. Somehow she knew this man was part of her past.

Staring into the mirror, trying to get her headband on just right, she knew there was no use denying the truth. From the second she had seen him from across the room, she had known he was the man who had haunted her dreams for so long, the man who had inspired her *Dragon's Law* games in the first place. But this was no game.

"Relax," she encouraged the frightened reflection in the mirror. All she had wanted was a weekend fling, not a date with destiny or anything that may upset her newly ordered, boring life.

Her hands shook as she tried one last time to get the ring of flowers to stay put on top of her overly curly hair. Pinning it into place, she took in a deep breath. So what if he was the guy from her dream? It didn't matter anyway. She wasn't the first person in the world to have dreams about strangers and then meet them.

But she couldn't pass this off as some weird cosmic accident. There was far more to her meeting of her dream man than just accidental destiny. And now her plans for a sexathon this weekend were going to be hindered by her good sense.

She would have thrown herself across the bed in defeat, but her fairy wings would have been crushed and three hundred dollars would have gone down the drain. They had survived the flight and she certainly wasn't going to mess them up just because of the self-doubt that wouldn't leave her alone.

Maybe he wouldn't even be at the masquerade. Maybe he had disappeared and had gone somewhere else to pick on another fairy or pixie and leave her to herself. She knew this would never happen. He had known her, too. So he may not have said the words, she saw the recognition sweep across his face when the cover for her new game was revealed. He felt the connection and knew that there was more to his being here than coincidence. She'd be willing to bet her next royalty check on it.

Still, he had conceded, had smiled and let her go when she suggested they meet later. Even though his eyes had held an intense look of something that may have been desire, he had let her slip away.

Then there was the damned necklace. The chain had managed to wind itself in her hair, and the clasp had gotten stuck. It was going to take an extra set of hands to get the thing unhooked unless she planned to cut a chunk out of her hair.

"Everything will be okay," she whispered to herself as she squared her shoulders and prepared once more to go downstairs, into the world of fairies and elves, to try to pretend like she wasn't looking over her shoulder for the man who very well could be the dragon in her video games.

She vowed to be on alert. Now that she knew Leland was in New Orleans she could work to avoid him. Pressing the elevator button, she steadied her nerves once more. Salvation was downstairs, she just knew it. All she had to do was find him.

Setting her shoulders into the most confident position she could manage, she turned sideways to go out her hotel room. The wings were cute, but they sure were in the way!

Gypsy music greeted her as she entered the ballroom. She almost expected to become lost among the ringing of tambourines. Instead, she saw a swirl of color and costumes wilder than any she had seen earlier in the day. Most of the revelers were masked, making it impossible to know who was who beneath the feathers, sequins and false noses.

Some of the partygoers wore elaborate, winged costumes while others wore vampire capes and witches' robes. Still others were dressed in more traditional elfin costumes. Her fairy wings were smaller than some, thank God, and made it easy enough to weave through the crowd to the back wall where the temporary bar was set up.

She had never felt the need to consume so much alcohol in her whole life. Everything about tonight screamed the need to calm her nerves. Her entire body pulsed with the possibility that she was teetering on the edge of something she couldn't quite define.

Her hand unconsciously went to the necklace still resting around her throat. She swore it was forcing her feet to move forward because they certainly weren't moving of her own volition. The crowd became a dizzying frenzy around her as she all but collapsed into the back of a tall, masked reveler. When he turned and looked down at her, his lips turning up in a smile, her heart stopped in her throat.

Okay, so she couldn't see his face beneath the leather mask, but she knew it was Damon. He had kept his bargain and was here tonight to finish what they had started earlier. Without a word, he held out his hands and waited as she stumbled into them, having been prodded forward by a dancing couple behind her.

As soon as he drew his arms around her, pulling her into his circle, she knew she would ask him up to her room. Every protest and warning she may have entertained earlier died. Nothing mattered outside of looking deep into his eyes and seeing her own reflection there. Okay, so maybe it wasn't the smartest line of thinking, but she knew instinctively that she was safe with him.

A wave of courage and bravado washed over her as she looked up at him, unable to do anything other than smile and join him in the mad dance that was swirling around them, intoxicating them with the movement of three hundred dancers.

"Do you know who I am, Kira?" he whispered against her hair, barely loud enough for her to hear above the music.

"Mmm. No." She snuggled against him, lost in the strange sensations assaulting her body. The necklace around her neck seemed to hum and pulse, feeding her images of another time and place, somewhere far away but so close she could almost touch.

"I am the one who will grant your wishes."

"I'd like that."

"No, I am here to give you the thing you need the most."

"So you're a djinn then?"

"No."

"Then what kind of costume is that?"

"Costume?"

"Yeah. Who are you pretending to be?"

"There is no need to pretend. I am who I say, and I am here to do what I say will. So tell me what you need, what you wish, and I will give it to you."

He was too serious. This was supposed to be a game, another of her little adventures into the world of the unreal. But Damon had stopped moving and his arms felt tight around her as he held on the dance floor, his eyes cutting into hers as if her answer could be his salvation.

"I need air." Pulling away as quickly as possible, she fled into the crowd. This was all too much, too soon. There was no way she was going to bring him up to her room, even if everything inside her wanted it.

Pushing open the patio doors, she stepped out into the night where the overflow from the party had gathered to cool off or to enjoy the billions of stars gathered overhead.

She wasn't the type to have a one-night stand. No matter how badly she wanted it, no matter how much she knew a night, or a weekend, with Damon could change her life. Closing her eyes tightly, she fought back tears and wished she were woman enough to take charge of her life and do something for a change. Take a chance. God, if ever there was a chance that needed taking, it was Damon.

She wasn't looking where she was going, a danger considering how much of her past seemed to be lurking around at this convention. With Constance and Leland here, it seemed as if her secret could be revealed to anyone. And she would once again be a girl from nowhere, a freak with no identity save for the one she had created.

"Going somewhere?"

Shit. This night was just going from bad to worse. And speaking of worse, Leland looked as if he had seen better days. She had only seen him a few hours ago, but he looked as if he had been hitting the bottle hard, and maybe it was even hitting back.

"Leland." She straightened her shoulders as he approached and tried not to cringe when his hand wrapped around her upper arm. He led her to the edge of the patio.

"I need to talk to you. You never called me." His voice was edgy, to say the least. It was like there was something up with him that she couldn't quite put her finger on.

"I've been busy."

"I know. With that weirdo."

"Who are you talking about?"

"It doesn't matter." He shook his head wildly, taking on the look of a mad wolf about to attack. "I need your blood."

That was all it took for her to jerk her arm out of his hand. "You're crazy. Look, I don't know what's going on with you, but…"

"Where did you get that necklace?" His bloodshot eyes glared at the charm around her neck. A shaky finger reached out to touch it and then recoiled as if it had been burned.

"At a pawn shop. What does it matter?"

"Does it always make that noise?"

God, he *was* losing it. She had never seen his eyes look so wild. His face was flushed red as if he had been running a marathon, and his hands shook as he reached for her again.

"Leave me alone." She swiped at his hand to no avail. Before she could move it closed around her throat and pulled her flush against his chest.

"I need to talk to you, but I can't do it while this thing is humming so loudly." His voice was steady, like a madman who was slowly trying to prove his sanity.

"Let go of me," she managed at the same time his hand moved from her neck. Just when she thought he was going to reclaim his sanity, he reached up and pulled the necklace from her neck, taking with it a wad of her hair. "Shit! What'd you do that for?" *Damn, that hurt!*

"I need your DNA. This should do."

The pain at the base of her skull seemed to move forward to her temples and then radiate down to her throat and chest. Before she knew it, it was difficult to breathe. The fever, a fever she hadn't known in a very long time, was back. She could feel it move through her body and stake its claim on her cells. Something inside her was changing. And it had nothing to do with having a few hairs yanked out. She'd done enough of that in the past with her hairbrush. No, this was something different. This was…

Laced with memories. They all started at the base of her skull and then throbbed when they reached her shoulder, where her wound once more felt open and raw. There was a man standing in front of her, his long dark hair falling forward, framing his glowing red eyes, eyes that were filled with anger. A growl erupted from his throat as he sprang forward. Someone else caught her and pushed her to the side. Her body collapsed against something she couldn't define.

The two faces above her morphed into something else, into something that looked suspiciously like the dragons in her video game. She tried to grab something, anything, to help steady her body as she felt herself fall. She didn't even have to look up to know he was behind her, and when his hands closed around the backs of her arms and he pulled her against him, there was no fear. She was safe with him.

Damon had come for her.

"I am looking for a pixie. Perhaps one I have offended. Do you know where I may locate one?" His smooth Transylvanian accent washed across her as he spoke.

"Help me," she managed, knowing he was the only one who could help her.

"Kira, what's wrong?" he turned her in his arms and placed a palm to her forehead. "The fever has you. It's his bite. It infected you."

"Nobody bit me."

"Mace bit you. Six years ago. He bit you and then forced you into a dark abyss." He pushed her hair out of her face.

"No. Damon. Take me to my room. I need…"

"You need me. Your body needs me, Kira. His DNA has mixed with yours and now you feel the change as it takes place on Tyr. Where is the necklace? It will help you."

"Necklace?" Nothing he was saying made any sense. He was speaking as if he knew her, and she still wasn't convinced this was anything more than a dream.

"The amulet you wear. My amulet. Where is it?"

"Leland."

"Tambourne," the word was said with clear disgust, but she didn't have time to contemplate how Damon and Leland knew one another. "Come, Kira. I will help you. I know you feel this thing between us."

The world was cloudy as her feet started moving again. "What thing?"

"The bond we share, you and I know one another."

"No." It wasn't possible for her to know him. Sure, he looked familiar, but surely she would remember him if they shared a bond.

"You know me, Kira. Close your eyes and place your hand here." He guided her hand to his chest as the world seemed to stop spinning. "Remember all those times I came to you in your dreams. Remember the time we spent together…" his voice broke with unspoken words, unspoken whispers she knew would be the death of her.

Fog filled her head. "They were only dreams."

"No, Kira. They were not dreams. You know deep down that they were not. You feel it. Those are your memories."

"No."

"Yes. Let me prove it to you. Do you feel steady now?"

She nodded. Surprisingly, she did feel as if she could walk without leaning into him. But, just in case, she leaned on him as they moved.

"Good. Where is your room? I need to show you something. I need to show you why you need me." His words echoed in her head even as he pulled her toward the elevator.

* * * * *

She wasn't really doing this. Her teeth wrapped around her bottom lip as she bit into it hard, trying to wake herself up from this crazy fantasy. Just because the man looked like a god did not mean she had to take him up to her room. She couldn't deny the way her pussy clenched and creamed just looking at him. When had a man ever had that kind of effect on her?

Catching a glimpse of his profile, trying not to stare too hard as the elevator climbed up the fourteen floors to her room, she watched as the muscles in his jaw clenched. He hadn't said a word since they entered the elevator, hadn't given any indication of the desire he had shown on the dance floor. Her heart sank a little as she wondered if he'd changed his mind. This wasn't how wild affairs were supposed to begin.

She wanted to say something to break the silence. Instead, she stood there, her arms folded around her, waiting for him to acknowledge her. Her lips felt dry and the champagne had gone to her head by the time the doors opened and he turned to her and smiled. The sinking feeling in her gut warned her that she was about to get in over her head. She shook off the thoughts of rationale. Tonight was not a night for rational thinking. It was a night for hot sex. And the hotter, the better.

"This is it."

"Your room?" He wrinkled his brow, as if confusion had set in.

"Yeah. My room."

He stared out into the hallway, as if he wasn't sure if he should follow her or not. She wouldn't beg. If he stayed in the elevator she would go to her room alone and probably spend the rest of the night kicking herself for her stupidity. To her surprise, he stepped out behind her just as the doors began to close. They quickly reopened, allowing room for his broad shoulders to pass through the threshold. She finally let out the breath she had been holding.

"Just let me get my key." She bent down to pull the key from her boot. When she did, his arms circled her waist, pulling her flush against him, pushing her wings aside with the motion, causing her backside to make contact with the hard muscles of his thighs. His penis pressed into the small of her back, warning her of his arousal. As his heated breath brushed against the back of her neck, his hand reached around to grasp her breasts. Her breath hung in her throat as his words grazed across her skin.

"I can feel your heat." The words sent a shiver down her back as they caressed her delicate skin.

God, she could melt against him. The man could read a cereal box and sound sexy. She tried to still her shaking hand, tried to force the key card into the slot, but her fingers refused to move. His hand closed over hers, taking the key and sliding it into place. "Thanks," she managed, though her voice had gotten lost somewhere between her throat and her lips.

"Come." He pushed the door open and she followed behind him. He had clearly taken charge of things once more. Doubt trickled through her, but she swallowed it, reminding herself that this was exactly why she had come to New Orleans in the first place, to have an affair and to forget the past. That had seemed so simple just a few hours ago.

Damon dominated the room, dwarfing everything with his sheer size. God, how had she ever thought she could handle a man like this? And the awkward silence was back, as if his mind were ten million miles away instead of on the woman who would probably hand her soul over to him if he asked for it. It had been far too long since she had been touched.

"Your room," he said. Hands on hips, he stood with his legs slightly parted, his crotch holding the most magnificent bulge she had ever seen.

"Yes." She licked her lips. It was now or never. "Do you want a drink?" She had to do something with her hands or die from anticipation. Pulling the wings from her back and placing them across the table, she walked to the mini bar.

"No, Kira. I do not want a drink." As his body began to move, she shrank against the wall, wondering if the pleasure from the heated look he shot would be enough to kill her or merely wound her. Either way, she knew she was about to find out.

"Well, what do you want, then?" Her voice shook as she tried again to still her pounding heart. He was standing inches away now, his hands clenched into fists at his sides. Those same warnings that had rung out earlier practically screamed to her now. He was a stranger and she had brought him to her room because he looked good.

No, that was not it exactly. She had brought him here because he looked like the man in her dreams, the one who had inspired her dragon video games where the princess holds the key to saving her man and his kingdom. Kira was no princess, though, and this man reeked of danger. Still, she couldn't help the fierce drumming of her heart as it beat in time with her pulsing pussy as he took the final step toward her, pinning her against the wall with his commanding frame.

"I want the charm." The words sounded as if they could barely push through his lips the second before he fell against her. "I need the charm, and you need it too, from the looks of you. We have to find Tambourne. But first, we have to end this ache, this fever, before it consumes us both."

Placing her hands between them, bracing herself for what may come next, she never imagined how hot his skin would feel or how vacant his eyes suddenly looked. He stumbled forward as he tried to right himself. Her arms were no match for his strength as he pressed her into the wall, pushing the breath from her chest.

"I need you," he whispered, his voice barely audible.

"I know you." She reached out to touch his face, visions from her past swirling around her, closing in on her. "I mean, I remember your face, but there's so much I don't know, so much I can't…"

"Shh. Don't try too hard. It will all come back to you."

"You said I was bitten. Someone named Mace?"

"You don't remember Mace?"

"No. All I remember is your face. You, smiling down at me. Who are you?"

"Your destiny. Once. Now come to me."

"No. My head is so foggy…"

"It will clear. You need me, as I need you."

"Damon…"

"Touch me, Kira. Touch me and allow me to help you recall what we had before it was taken from us. Let me love you tonight."

Chapter Four

There was no controlling the animal lust. He had had every intention of demanding she return the amulet and then leaving her be, but Tambourne had won this round, taking the amulet. Now they were both in danger of becoming consumed by the fire that raged inside them. Mace's bite had infected her just as his blood affected him. And, tonight, when his hand brushed hers, it was as if it had moved of its own accord, without direction from his brain. That was when he had lost the little restraint he had left. The dragon had won the battle of wills and was now threatening to escape its hiding place. The fever had taken over his body and now he had no choice but to fall into her lips first and do that which nature intended.

Her eyes were green with flecks of blue that had been brought out, no doubt, by her light blue costume, but right now they smoldered with a combination of fear and desire, desire winning out. When his head lowered to hers, just before their lips touched, her eyes smoldered with golden fire, sending her desire straight to his core, drawing him in like a moth to a flame. And he was lost in her gaze somewhere, swimming for air. For a moment, she was his Kira. And may the gods damn him for it, but he needed her!

Her mouth tasted as if the nectar of the gods resided there. The dragon within him growled from beneath his skin, warning him that he must take her tonight or else lose control of the beast. Damon knew he had no choice in the matter, not that he wanted one. The only thing he wanted right now was to part her pink lips, to slide his tongue into her body and to love her with a wild abandon. But there were rules to consider, consequences to his actions. And taking her would not come without a price even though his time was running out and the need to mate was upon him, fierce and demanding.

"What do you want?" His finger traced along her swollen bottom lip, which felt like satin beneath his callused touch. He had no right to her, none save for the fact that his amulet had chosen her. And the fact that he would die without her.

"I don't know." Confusion flashed in her eyes as she spoke. Then, a slow, lazy smile spread across her lips. "I want you."

"There are things you do not know about me. Things you do not yet recall."

"I don't want to know anything about you. I just want you."

The words tore through him even as the dragon reacted to the scent of her sweet cunt as it rose up to greet him, her cream obviously preparing her for loving him. He had known her body would be ready, had known she would smell like the heavens, but he never thought that she would be so brutally honest in her pursuit.

He pulled her flush against him, watching her eyes flicker with golden desire once more. Pressing his leather-covered penis against her stomach, he watched the slow smile cross her lips once more. It did not matter what she wished to know. The amulet had chosen her, and she would probably live to regret this night.

The dragon whispered low and long, his growl trapped somewhere in Damon's throat as Kira reached up to brush her fingers along his lips. He opened his mouth, snarling, taking two fingers between his teeth and biting down gently. She gasped and shook against him. It did not matter what fantasy she had in mind. Tonight was about need, and about him regaining control before the darkness enveloped him and destroyed them both.

"Tonight you shall have me," she purred.

Guilt snaked up his back. If he took Kira without explaining to her the pact they were about to make with their bodies, he would be no better than the thief he had been the night he had kidnapped her so long ago.

He should leave her there, walk away quietly and leave her to her new life. Surely there were willing, warm bodies downstairs, bodies that would gladly spread their thighs for him. But there were laws, again, laws he had no control over, but which controlled his every movement. But he feared that the fever raging inside her was just as strong as that which drove him. Leaving her here would cause her to choose another mate, something he would not allow.

If he took a woman to bed tonight, it was not just for a night but for the entire period of the dark moon. If Kira took a lover, the same rules would apply. As a stranger in a strange land, that prospect was monumentally important. Mating with her, letting her back into his life was the reason he was here, but taking her here and now was more complicated than he wished. Mace would take the throne unless he was there to stop him, and he needed Kira to help him toward that end. But if Kira returned, would she choose him or hate him?

The sweet smell of her hair wafted up to him, reminding him of exotic flowers from home. Her soft skin still lingered in his mind just as her lips and their willingness to crush against his threatened to force his hand once more. This was the one he wished to mate with, to take back to his home, to make promises that he knew he couldn't keep, promises she was unable to keep.

Her white teeth closed around her bottom lip, which was slightly red and swollen from his kiss. The thoughts racing through her head were too many, too quickly discarded for him to focus on any of them. Only one thought rang out above all else. *Save me.*

He smiled, knowing the truth. She needed saving as much as he did.

He allowed her scent to penetrate his brain, to work its way into his system, branding him deep inside with the memory of how it felt to be this close to another creature, something he never did out of want and always did out of necessity. The spirit guides joined the dragon's chant now, warning him that things were about to change, that his fate had been to come to Earth all along, to come to New Orleans and find this creature whose beauty and sadness defied all logic, the woman who had simultaneously destroyed them both.

* * * * *

Kira tried to relax against him, tried to ignore the fact that in three tiny seconds, his lips had ignited a fire in her that now threatened to rage out of control. Her lifelong fear of the unknown had been forgotten in her momentary brush with his lips. He could be anyone, but tonight, he would be hers. Fate had sent her a challenge. *Are you woman enough to do what you want, Kira?* She feared the answer.

Her hands ached to run up and down his back, to feel the muscles there flex and relax as they moved their bodies in a slow rhythm that had nothing to do with the music playing in the background. It was as if the entire world had melted away and there were only the two of them. Thoughts swam through her head as she drank in his rich scent. He smelled like everything a man was supposed to smell like all wrapped into one package. He felt like everything a man was supposed to feel like.

Wrapping her arms around him even tighter, she gave in to the dream. If she was dreaming, she sure had one hell of an imagination. His fingertips pressed on her lower back, and her abdomen came into contact with his penis. Hard, very much aroused, waiting for her. Her breath caught in her throat as she looked up at him. He seemed oblivious to the fact that he had a hard-on, and she suddenly hoped to all things holy that he wasn't soft.

"Tell me your wishes," he whispered into her hair, sending another wave of delight through her body. He was playing on a fantasy just as everyone else here was. And why not go along with it?

"Why do you want to know?" The urge to resist was still strong.

Was that a laugh? "I wish to know all about the woman who will take me to bed tonight."

She stiffened in his arms and tried to pull away, turning her back to him, but he held her close. Alarms went off inside her head. Men could not be trusted, especially not gorgeous strangers who seemed to know all the right things to say. This was a setup of some kind, though she had no idea who would want to set her up, or why. And she didn't understand why she couldn't pull away.

"Don't turn around, Kira." His words held a warning she couldn't understand. He could feel the unspoken questions pounding inside her with every wild beat of her heart. Still, she obeyed, to his surprise.

She stood before him, her back to him, her long hair brushing against the hand he had on her waist. Her breath was hung somewhere in her throat as he listened to the turmoil inside her body. She was not accustomed to taking men into her room, but Damon swore he was not just another man, and she knew she was no ordinary woman.

"What are you doing?"

He had done nothing save for run his hands along her shoulders and down her arms, yet it set her entire body on fire. "Close your eyes," he whispered.

"Your hands are so hot." She rolled her neck as she spoke, inviting him to touch the delicate flesh in the crook where her shoulder and neck met. He obliged, running his long, fingers along her skin, the resulting sensations heavenly.

"Mmmm," was his only response to her observation.

"You aren't ill, are you?"

"No, I am not ill. Don't turn around. It is you who are making my hands so heated. I am feeding off your energy. You are nervous, no?"

"I don't think we should do this."

"Why should we not? Do you not want me?"

"I want you all right. But there's really no point in this. It's just meaningless sex."

She slipped from his grasp and he held his breath firmly in his chest. If she turned around, she would see the long nose, the red eyes—the dragon breaking free of its master. He waited for her to turn, to run in horror. Instead, she stood perfectly still, as if she were waiting for encouragement, waiting for him to take charge.

There was no need to answer. The energy seeped into his fingertips as he touched her. It had been so long since she had been touched this way, too long since he had touched her.

Her words ached as they made their way into his chest. He felt the pain behind them, the reasons why Kira had not been loved in so long. She was a woman with no past, yet he knew differently. He could give her the answers she sought, but those answers could once again destroy him. "It is not meaningless to me."

"I bet you say that to all the girls."

"Lean against me and let me love you."

She swayed before her body fell against his, her back pressed against his chest, her soft bottom pressed against the need between his thighs. Smoke rings blew from his nose just before he inhaled her scent. She smelled like wild orchids. When his lips made contact with the back of her neck, avoiding the roses, the dragon receded, knowing he would feast tonight.

"I want to see you." His breath hung in his throat as she turned, and he stood there helpless, hoping he once more looked like a man. "There, that's better." Her fingers traced along his jawline, forcing his heartbeat to quicken as her touch lingered too long over his lips.

"Kira…" the word was part sacred plea and part utter desperation. He needed her in a way he could not begin to explain. Every breath he took in her presence solidified his need as he drank in her velvety scent.

"Shh…let me." She removed his robe slowly before her head dipped down to his chest where her tiny mouth closed over his nipple. "I want to explore your body, to bring you pleasure. Will you let me do that, Damon?"

Willingly. Gods, yes, he would love to have her soft hands on him, caressing him, kneading his flesh into a thousand tiny explosions. But the sadness that reflected in her eyes told him she needed him for much more than a moment's pleasure. Not only did she wish to please him, but she wished to end the aching in her chest, an ache that Damon knew all too well. Whatever had happened to her, she was once again the innocent woman whose love he had once won. Everything inside him wished for a moment to turn back time and make her his.

"I will let you do whatever you wish to me."

Her eyes lit up at the prospect as she began pushing him toward the bed. "Good. I had hoped you would say that."

Chapter Five

Kira's boldness seemed to come out of nowhere. There was something about the way his words caressed her skin that made her want to please him, want to touch him. Her desire for him became a driving need that pulsed through her skin, hot and urgent, as if it had a stake in their joining.

When the backs of his legs made contact with the bed, she stopped against him, reveling once more in the feel of his body pressed against hers. She wondered how long it had been since she had loved a man and felt loved in return. Had she loved Damon before? Everything was still so foggy, so cluttered in her mind, she still couldn't remember anything save for the fact that she knew his face. Damon was a stranger to her, but at the same time he was the only person in the world she felt a connection to. Something in his eyes reflected the same need she felt deep in her soul. It was as if they were destined to be together, a thought she knew was nothing but a childish fancy. Still, he had done in a few hours what no man had done in years. He made her want him.

"You are wearing way too many clothes." She smiled as she ran her hands along his chest and then moved lower to his trousers.

He smiled down at her as she began unbuttoning the pants, trying to remain focused on the moment and trying not to worry about tomorrow or the day after. What she needed right now was the man whose scent was driving her fingers forward, forcing her to want with a need so strong it practically throbbed between her legs.

The man from her dreams stood before her. She was certain of it now. God, this man was absolute perfection from the cut of his abs to his bulging pecs. He swore he wasn't a model but there wasn't much else he could be unless he was a warrior of old, somehow trapped here in her time. Ordinary men did not look like this. They did not have eyes that looked right into her soul and didn't have a smile that practically melted her on contact. And they didn't drive the need like he did.

When his arms surrounded her and pulled her to him, she was lost. His fingers moved to untie the back of her dress before sliding it down her back. Before she could think to protest, her boots and stockings were also removed, leaving her there in her lacy bra and panties. With a wicked smile, he took her bra clasp in his hand and slipped the fabric from her skin, exposing her breasts. Finally, his hands slid down her thighs, removing the last stitch of covering with them. He smiled and then wrapped his arms around her.

She clung to him, hoping he would show her the way out of this maze of emotions that threatened to overwhelm her. She didn't want a man like him for a night, someone who looked and acted like a knight in shining armor. No, she wanted him for all time, even though she knew that was something a woman like her could never have.

Self-doubt reared its ugly head as her body slid against his, as his mouth captured hers in another of his searing kisses, the kind that ignited her all the way to her toes. Tears stung the backs of her eyes when the intensity became too much, when his tongue became too hot, too demanding, when the tiny voice in her head warned that this was just a dream.

"I don't think I can do this," the words came out as a breathless, empty plea. When she met his eyes, she knew he was too far gone already, having feasted on her mouth.

"Please, Kira, I must have you."

He rolled over, placing her beneath him. For a second, he stared deep into her eyes, and she swore his glowed red. When his mouth came down upon her neck, his teeth sinking into her flesh, threatening to send her to orgasm with that act alone, her resistance left her body. To hell with tomorrow. He was here right now.

"Damon," she moaned against him.

"Are you wet for me?"

Yes, she was wet for him, in spite of her insecurities. And she swore if he touched her there, the heat from his body would cause her flesh to sizzle. He hadn't reached for her yet, hadn't groped or grasped like she had expected. Instead, he seemed to be teetering on the edge of control as his mouth worked its way down to her chest.

His hands closed over her breasts, forcing a gasp from her throat. She longed to be naked beneath him, to have his hot skin pressed against her, to have his cock riding deep inside her. "Please, Damon."

"Please what?"

"I want you to love me."

His hands never left her body as they stroked her sides, her waist and her breasts. His fingers closed around one nipple and then the other, giving each a light squeeze as she shuddered against the bed, all thoughts of protest completely abandoned.

"I'm going to love you," he warned when his lips brushed against her ear. "I'm going to show you exactly how you should be loved. I'm going to take these into my mouth." His hand caressed her breasts before moving lower to brush across her abdomen. "Then I'm going to go lower. I'm going to run my tongue along your thighs. When you think you'll die from anticipation, I'm going to take your tiny clit between my teeth and pull until you come. Has anyone ever done that to you before?"

She shivered her answer, unable to still the quaking deep inside. Her pussy clenched in response to his words, willing his hands to move lower now. Her juices dripped out, fully preparing her for his body. God, she had yet to see his cock, but feeling it pressed against her stomach was almost more than she could stand.

"Then, Kira, I'm going to run my tongue along your folds and drink your juices as they spill out of your body. I'm going to watch your cunt as it trembles and vibrates, awaiting my cock. Then, when I'm sure you are ready, I'm going to place my cock right here." He moved to accentuate his point. For almost a full second, his cock pressed against her opening. She barely had time to arch her back, to beg him to enter her, before he moved away.

"You'll stretch for me as I fill you. And when I come inside you, you will know that you are mine. I am going to brand you tonight, Kira. No man shall ever touch you again."

The words hid a warning, one that she was too horny to understand. His woman forever? Sounded good to her. There could be no harm in a little love play, a little fantasy.

When his tongue began trailing its way down her body, following the path he had promised, her hands fisted into the covers. The white cotton became her salvation as he dipped his head low, taking her clit between his teeth before torturing it with his tongue, which flicked back and forth across her most sensitive spot in a way that had her practically screaming beneath her panting breath. Waves of delight swept over her as he threatened to push her over the edge. She was blinded by need, by desire.

Her nails scraped along his back, surely drawing blood. His movements felt so controlled, so calculated. Finally, when she thought she would surely die from the need, his cock rested against her pussy, preparing to finally give her exactly what she needed.

She swore she heard voices urging him forward but his mouth had destroyed her sanity. It could have been the air conditioner for all she knew. Her pussy quivered, begging him once more to enter her. Her teeth caught her bottom lip for fear of screaming, of dying from the sensation. And, finally, he entered her.

His cock moved slowly at first, sinking into her inch by inch until he was finally buried deep inside her. For a second he didn't move. His breath, hot and ragged, brushed against her neck.

God, if he moved any slower, she would die! Each thrust took an excruciatingly long time. He pulled out slowly, removing all but the head of his penis before pushing himself back into her, taking his time with each motion.

Her hips refused to be still as she looked up at him. His eyes were focused on their bodies, on the joining of flesh against flesh. The erotic sight must have pleased him because he continued to watch even as his intensity increased. He answered her thrusting with renewed vigor, driving himself into her harder, deeper.

"You should see how amazing you look. Your body opens for me, demands that I take you. Your sweet, soft pussy loves my cock, loves to be tormented by it. Do you love it, Kira?"

"Yes."

"Do you want to see?"

"God, yes."

"Next time, love. Next time I take you, you shall see every tiny motion. I want you to see how you open for me, how your muscles squeeze and pulse, how your clit grows large. I want you to see what I do to you."

Oh, God, she was going to come. The words combined with the sensations building deep inside her body and then erupted into wave after wave of pure ecstasy. He didn't slow as she came around him, milking his cock. He increased his movements, but now, instead of watching their bodies join, he looked deep into her eyes and sank his hands into her hair, forcing her head still, forcing her to watch him.

"Look at me, Kira. Look at me while I love you."

She tried to focus on him, tried to still her pounding heart, tried to overcome the blinding rush of sensations that shattered her body and forced her to lie there, whimpering, clinging to him as he arched his back and shot his hot seed into her body.

"Oh, God!" The words were ripped from her throat as his heat shot against her womb, branding her, as he had promised. Never, ever would she be the same. And never would she forget the stranger who had given her this gift.

"Kira," the word caressed her neck. "My sweet Kira."

* * * * *

There was no explanation for the thousands of emotions that assaulted him as he pulled himself from her body. He had not meant to love her, yet at the same time, he knew he could not resist her. Once again, he had taken Kira like a thief in the night. Having her in his arms again made him want nothing more than to stay with her forever. As she lay wrapped in his arms, the earth and the heavens felt as if they had aligned to smile down upon them. He could not keep her, though, yet he knew he couldn't leave her behind. She belonged with him on Tyr. But to go back there and to bring her home would open them both up to heartbreak. They had loved for an entire moon period before her betrayal. He swallowed hard, knowing he was no innocent in the betrayal. His deceit had forced her to run into Mace's arms.

She arched her back and tilted her head up so that her smile graced him. If he were able to choose a life mate, it would be her, his Kira. *His Kira*. The thought sent warmth through his body and caused his heart to beat with renewed vigor. The choice had already been made.

"What are you thinking?" Her voice, smooth as spun silk, washed over him. He pulled her closer, wishing he could sink his skin into hers, wrap himself around her and completely become one with her sweetness.

"I am thinking about many things." It was the truth. There was no way to tell her what he needed to say, no way to make her understand. *Tell her the truth*, the voice inside his head warned. *No. Not yet,* he countered. He would tell her, but not today.

"Care to share them with me?" Her soft fingertips brushed against his jaw, which was uncustomarily covered with a dark beard.

"I shall when the time is right. For now, I just wish to love you."

Her breasts rose and fell as her fingers worked their way into his hair.

"And I wish for a bath."

She smiled and then pulled herself from his arms. He watched as she rose from the bed and made her way to the door, which shut the bedroom off from the bathing room. When her hand touched the doorknob, she turned and gave a little smile, bringing his cock back to life with that tiny motion. "You coming?"

The tub was large enough for both of them, he realized upon entering the room. She was already bent over the tub, her long hair dancing against her back as she poured a bluish liquid into the water. Steam rose, enveloping him as soon as the door closed. In the mist she looked like a goddess, her slender frame illuminated by the glowing bulbs and candlelight.

"Get the lights, will you?"

He fumbled with the wall switch before finally shutting off the overhead light, leaving her bathed completely in candlelight. He swallowed hard and his cock jerked in reaction to her.

"That's better, don't you think?"

Kira stood and turned to face him, her face angelic as she looked up at him. "Kira," the word was like a sacred oath as it spilled from his lips and caused her to smile.

"Come here. Let me bathe you."

She held out her hand as if he were a child, and he not-so-innocently took hers, allowing her to lead him the three steps to the tub. When his feet first made contact with the bubbly water the steam increased, rising of its own volition. Contact with water often caused steam to rise in the air, as his skin was hotter than that of most men.

Kira's breasts swayed as she stepped into the tub behind him. Rather than sitting in the water as he had thought she would do, she sat on the edge of the tub, her body just within reach. He watched her slender arm as it extended to take a sponge from the shelf. His body stiffened as he watched her move, he felt like a voyeur to a goddess' secret rituals.

"I never expected you," she confessed, and he felt how the words pained her as she finally sank into the water with him.

"And I never expected you."

"I feel like you came here looking for me or something." Her hand reached out to stroke his chest as she spoke, but rather than touching him with her satiny hands, she ran the soapy sponge along his chest, tangling the suds into the hair covering his muscles. There was a slight sadness in her tone and even more in her demeanor.

"Does that make you sad, Kira? That I would have come all this way in search of you?"

"No, not sad. It just makes all this even more unbelievable. I mean, why would you come here for me?" She didn't look up at him as she spoke, which forced him to take her chin and raise it. Her innocent eyes were glazed over with longing and fear.

"Why would you not believe it?"

"Look, let's not talk any more, okay? Just let me wash you. Relax. There's so much I'd like to do to you and we've only got a little bit of time left."

The thought of fleeting time with Kira pained his heart. She avoided eye contact again as she continued to slide the sponge across his chest, not fully concentrating on any one area, brushing across his tender nipples as if they did not catch fire every time she touched him.

He had to tell her the truth.

Kira bit her bottom lip as she tried to concentrate on Damon's body. Tears stung the backs of her eyes, but she refused to let them fall. She had never been this close to heaven and she'd be damned if she let it go without a fight. But how could she, Kira from nowhere, hold onto a man like Damon, someone who could clearly have any woman he wanted?

His hand closed around her wrist, stopping any further movement. A tiny whimper escaped her throat before she could conceal it. When she looked up into his eyes, they glowed golden, filled with desire.

There were no words between them. There was no need. Something about her body responded to him in a primal way, a way that needed no communication save for his hands on her. When he pulled her to him she flattened her hand against his chest, at first to keep herself from falling, but then it was to keep herself from melting into him.

But he didn't kiss her as she thought he would. Instead, he sat there, his arms wrapped around her waist, his cock pressed into her stomach. And he just looked at her as if he were trying to see something deep inside, trying to penetrate her soul with his gaze.

When his mouth finally closed over hers she felt the sensation all the way to her toes and knew she was drowning in him. There was no way to save herself from the sweet invasion as her mouth opened for him, allowing him access to all of her if he wished it.

The sponge dropped into the water, but she didn't feel it leave her hands as they twisted into his hair and pulled him closer to her. If she could have melted their bodies together and become one with this stranger, this man who, in less than twenty-four hours, had managed to penetrate her heart in a way no one else had ever done before, she would have.

"I want to love you, Kira," he whispered against her mouth.

"Hold on." She freed herself from his arms long enough to reach from the bubbly tub into the basket sitting nearby. Thank God for weird friends. One of the junior programmers had been certain Kira would need a bag of goodies for her trip and had graced her with waterproof lubricant as well as a few other treats.

"What's this?" He wrinkled his brow as she pulled the small vial from the basket and placed it onto the edge of the tub.

"It's help. You know, for me. To keep me wet." She could feel the blush rising in her temples. He seemed unaffected by her admission.

"I shall keep you plenty wet." It was part threat, part promise and something she knew he would be true to.

"I have no doubt about that." The breath left her body when he pulled her onto his lap, placing his hard cock against her swollen clit.

God, she ached for him, actually ached. She felt her walls spasm, urging her to move, to pull him into her body. Instead, she sat perfectly still, allowing him to move her as he wished.

"I love your body," he whispered against her neck. "I want to watch you pleasure yourself."

She froze.

"Kira, come for me. Show me how you can make yourself come."

"Damon, I…"

"Please. I wish it. I want you to sit on the edge of the tub and look into the mirror. I want you to show me."

The large mirror covering the wall behind the tub was something she hadn't counted on when she rented the room. She had never been one for looking at herself naked and now, in the presence of a veritable god, she found it even more difficult.

"I can't."

"Please. For me. Love yourself. Use your aids, whatever you call them. I want to watch you come."

The basket near the tub held more than the lubricant. He must have seen it earlier when she was preparing the bath. Her teeth closed on her bottom lip as she contemplated the man sitting before her. God, she wanted to make him happy. But more than that she wanted to see herself as he saw her. She wanted to watch herself come in the candlelight.

Swallowing her fear, she pulled herself up onto the edge of the tub, which was perfectly made for her bottom. Damon moved to the side, allowing her full view of the mirror. She couldn't do this. She stole a sideways glance at him as his hand moved to his cock, primed to stroke himself when she moved.

Squeezing her eyes shut, she moved her hand down her stomach as she spread her thighs. Her clit glistened in the candlelight, beckoning her when she opened her eyes and looked at herself. She tried not to see the extra layer of fat she had gained, tried not to notice how her breasts sagged when they were not being supported by the push-up bra. Damon was not focused on her flaws, though. She could tell by the way he focused on her. He didn't see all those things she hated about herself.

She watched in awe as he began stroking his cock.

Bracing herself with one arm, she leaned back and parted her nether lips with her free hand. At first, she stiffened, unaccustomed to having someone watch her while she pleasured herself. Her fingers began moving around her outer lips, lightly stroking at first. She tried to concentrate on her movements, tried not to focus on the flaws of her body as she touched herself.

When her fingers brushed against her clit, it reacted, causing the pressure to build within her body. It usually didn't take much to get herself off. She was accustomed to doing it quickly, coming and then going back to work. Tonight, she wanted to take it slowly, build herself up to a frenzy before coming and make it a show worth watching.

She leaned back and pulled the glass dildo from the basket. Damon seemed to fade into the background, the reason for her self-love but not part of the action. Everything faded away except her pussy and her hands. Again, bracing herself, she moved to the edge and spread her legs wide. Using the lubricant, she rubbed her clit then slid her fingers inside one at a time to make room for the large dildo. Finally, when she felt she was ready, she positioned it at her opening and took a deep breath before sliding it home.

Not interested in slow play, she slid it in as far as it would go then reached around with her other hand and began rubbing her clit as she moved the glass cock in and out of her pussy. The sound of her body fucking the cock rose up to greet her, blocking out all other sounds in the room.

"Oh, yeah," she moaned, no longer ashamed of her pleasure.

Her hand moved faster as she leaned further back and raised her pussy to meet the cock. She wasn't aware that Damon had moved until she felt his hands around her waist and his chest pressed against her back. He raised her so she could see herself as her pussy greedily took the cock in, no matter how hard her thrusts became.

Damon's fingers closed over her nipples while his breath brushed against her neck. She leaned into him, allowing her weight to rest on him while he remained in the shadows, watching her. The cock slid in and out of her pussy while her fingers worked feverishly, massaging the tender flesh that surrounded her clit. She knew how to touch herself, barely grazing her clit with her fingers, placing pressure on either side while she rubbed circles into her skin.

Her ass arched up again and she watched as her walls began to quake. The spasms were easy to see as her labia began to tremble and the skin between her cunt and her ass clenched and unclenched in utter abandonment.

"You are so beautiful." Damon's words washed over her as the orgasm hit, sending her over the edge, practically screaming in delight.

She thrust the cock into her pussy one last time, holding it in place, pushing it in as far as it would go while she rode out the wave of her orgasm. The next few seconds were a blur. Damon lifted her somehow and placed her onto the floor. She felt the dildo as he pulled it from her body. She was on all fours, her legs spread, awaiting his cock.

Without words he positioned himself at her opening, which was already creamed with longing. When he entered her it was swiftly and completely. Her pussy had already been stretched by the overly large dildo but Damon's cock stretched it even further, making her feel as if she'd never been touched. When she felt his balls rest against her labia she wiggled her ass, pressing him in even further.

His hands gripped her hips as he pulled her against him and then pushed her away. With every thrust, her moans rose to meet his, her ass thrust against his cock, her pussy begged for more. A growl erupted from his throat and she swore that in the mirror his square jaw elongated in a trick of light.

She was lost in her fantasy, lost in her orgasm. When she looked back his face appeared exactly as it had before, beautiful, masculine, the perfect representation of the hero from her game. Her pussy took his cock, never tiring of it as he continued to move inside her, slowly then quickly, his pace changing as he angled his cock against her g-spot and then moved away. The hard tile of the bathroom floor raked against her knees and caused her nipples to harden as they flattened against it when she was unable to hold herself off the floor. Resting her head on her hands, she lay there, her ass raised, her pussy open while Damon took everything he wanted from her.

When the next orgasmic wave hit her, she rose up on all fours then moved one hand around to close over her clit. This time when she came she felt his seed shoot inside her body and felt his frame quiver against her. Liquid heat spread through her as he clung to her, his hands in her hair, pulling her head back against him, using her as leverage in order to drive his cock further inside her.

They collapsed together on the floor. His ragged breathing joined hers and neither moved, neither spoke as they lay there tangled in one another. Finally, he stood and pulled her from the floor. Depositing her into the warm tub, he washed her body wordlessly. There was something sacred about what had happened between them, and she felt as if no words were needed for the ten thousand emotions raging inside her.

Could she love this man she didn't even know? What was required for love anyway? She had no past. All she had was right now, and she was afraid that wasn't enough.

* * * * *

Two nights after he had taken her prisoner, six and a half years before, she had challenged him beyond all reasoning. He remembered it now as she lay in his arms, and he knew he had to tell her the truth. They had been in his cave then, his hideaway from the world. He had taken her there to protect her from Mace, not realizing then how much danger he was placing her in.

Damon had groaned at the change in temperature as soon as he entered the cave. It snaked its way up his body, warning him of the battle to come. The night he kidnapped her he had injected her with a bit of his poison, a dragon aphrodisiac to subdue her. After it had worn off, she had been ready for battle. He'd closed his eyes and prepared for the blows he'd known she would inflict upon him since she was no longer susceptible to the desires of the flesh.

She came at him, weapon raised, ready to strike. Damon reacted, putting up his arm in defense, trying all the while to ignore the ache in his heart. He knew it was for the best that Kira react to him this way now that the poison had left her body. Taking her from her home lay upon him like a heavy weight, and her anger was nothing more than what he deserved. Kira attacked once more, her makeshift weapon dealing a blow to his face, tearing into his flesh.

"I know what you did to me, monster! Fight me!" she demanded, coming at him again.

"You know not what you ask!" He held out an arm, blocking the next blow. In doing so, the stick flew from her hand, leaving her with no weapon. She charged once more. "Beware little one," he warned, feeling the change upon him.

"I'll kill you," she warned. "You injected me with your poison to have your way with me."

"You did not object to my taking you. And I thought you said you knew little of dragon ways."

"I know enough. I was defenseless. You knew that, yet you took me anyway."

"You were willing."

"I was poisoned with your aphrodisiac, or whatever you want to call it. You forced me." Poison or not, Kira had wanted him. His blood boiled with her accusation.

"You know nothing of me," he threatened.

"I know you steal woman and eat children." Her eyes were furious, having fully recovered from the hypnotic spell of the evening before.

"Kira, I feel your anger." The pain gripped his chest. He couldn't control it. She had spilled his blood. It trickled down his face, found its way into his mouth. She continued her assault on his body with nothing more than her fists.

He was blinded, and the change was here. "Kira," he growled, the last human sound he could muster. He watched her eyes widen in horror as his face became that of the dragon. Once the dragon emerged the change came on quickly, uncontrollably. It had wanted her flesh from the second she came into his sight. Now, as she challenged it, fought it, Damon's ability to quell the beast was lost in the struggle. He looked down in horror as his hands became claws and his legs extended. The tail grew from his backside, completing the change, and the dragon emerged, hungry and longing for her flesh.

Kira stood still, apparently in shock from witnessing the change. When the dragon cry erupted from his throat, Damon's tail swished back and forth, threatening to knock her off balance, and pinned her against the wall.

She fumbled, trying to grasp anything that could be used as a weapon. Damon stalked forward, his eyes locked onto hers, his dragon feeding off the fear while the man fed off the energy.

Anger triggered the change, just as a threat to one's life did. When she spilled his blood his body reacted. And now she was facing the dragon in his full fury.

Damon breathed in the scent of her flesh. His talons opened her lips, holding her so that he could delve inside and taste even more of her sweetness. He could have fucked her as a dragon. He could have given her the beast's cock, but he knew it would have killed her. The dragon had her luscious body on his mind. And wanted it with a ferocity Damon couldn't explain.

He had been able to subdue the beast with a taste of her pussy, which had been enough to help him regain control. Her sweet nectar saved her life. Still, the beast wanted to be rewarded. It wanted to take her savagely and wanted her to fight him. Deep inside, Damon wanted her to fight him.

He steadied his breathing as the dragon began to fade. If he couldn't control the beast inside him he was no better than his brother. His every instinct wanted to mate with her as warrior and dragon but the man inside him knew he couldn't harm her. But Kira didn't know this as she looked up at him, a hint of fear in her eyes. As his hand once more became human, he gently pushed two fingers into her slit and watched her eyes glaze over. She let out a sharp gasp when he penetrated her. "I'm going to punish you now," he threatened, though the dragon had now rested its head. "I'm going to punish your pussy. Do you understand, Slayer?" he growled.

She nodded, still gasping and moaning.

"No, you don't understand. I'm going to take you in as many ways as I can imagine. And you are going to be my slave. And if you try to kill me again, I shall let the dragon fuck you and rip you in half. Do you understand?" The warning echoed on the air, but he knew it was nothing more than the words of an angry man who was battling his own beast. He'd never harm her, but in order to keep his heart intact he couldn't let her know that.

Unwilling to let her know how she affected him, Damon had flipped her over onto her knees. "Do not move," he hissed into her ear. His penis was already throbbing, already tortured just thinking of diving into her. And the beast was still there on the edge of his mind, taunting him with knowledge of how it could be between them if he could only take with no thoughts of harming her.

She was wetter than the dragon wanted. He wanted her dry, wanted to force himself into her, to rip her skin open the way she had ripped his face open. Damon closed his eyes and fought down the beast, determined not to let him win. When he opened them, her soft pink folds winked at him, opening and closing as she shifted, waiting, anticipating. Her juices coated her outer lips. As he blew out a warm breath, she quivered with delight. The dragon may have made her fear him but it had also turned her on.

Damon ran his fingers along her skin, waiting for her, wanting her to be ready for him. When she groaned and arched against him he gently slapped her opening, coating his hand with her juices. She gasped at the contact but then she wiggled her ass, inviting another rough touch. His hand struck against her again, gaining the same reaction. He continued his assault, slapping her pussy and being rewarded with her gasps, groans and wiggles.

She arched back, placing her folds into the air, inviting him in. Begging him to take her. Begging him to slide into her sweetness and pound them both to ecstasy. Her flesh was red from his assault. Still, it quivered, wanting more.

He grabbed her hips, positioning himself at her tiny opening. In one swift motion, he slid inside of her, all the way up to his balls. She spasmed around him, ground her hips into him.

"You want it rough, Slayer?"

She arched herself into him. He wound his hands into her hair, pulling her head back. With that as leverage, he pounded into her, pulling her hair, punishing her pussy.

His cock slid in and out. With each thrust inside of her he pushed deeper. He wanted to leave his mark on her. Come deep inside of her. Hurt her. Love her. Gods, what was happening to him?

Her juices coated him, dripping out of her.

"Please," she called. He couldn't see her face, but he could hear the emotion in her voice.

"Please what?" he tried to keep the brutal edge to his voice, but his heart was reacting to her.

She arched against him again. This time she squeezed with an intensity he thought he'd never recover from. "Please love me."

"Come for me, slave," he coaxed, barely able to keep himself from spilling inside her at her admission. *Love me.* What did she know of love?

Then she came, her body spilling its juices around his cock as she moaned. She twisted her hips, grinding herself into him, taking him to her deepest part. He felt his release building and he released her hair and slowly pulled out.

He wasn't ready to come yet.

"I love you."

Damon's back straightened as she said the words and her fingers fell from his face. This wasn't what he wanted to hear, but he knew the admission had been lingering there, just on the edge every time he took her. The days had melted away into a week, and he still hadn't left the confines of the cave for more than a few hours to hunt. His desire to challenge his brother had lessened, his mind having been clouded by their lovemaking.

"You do not love me," he grumbled, hoping his voice sounded convincing, knowing he could never be what she needed. The amulet was the key to everything. Only now that he had lost control did he realize how it enslaved him.

"Yes, I do."

"'Tis the poison." He wanted to release her naked body from his arms but was unable to move. She had captured him, ensnared him as surely as if she held him in chains.

"The poison?" She rose up on her elbow and looked into his eyes, the innocence that had been there days ago replaced by a wanton gaze.

"Yes. The poison. It entered your blood, making you think you love me. This is what happens when you mate with a dragon." She slid from his arms, making them feel cold, empty.

"What do you mean?" Her voice sounded as if she were on the verge of tears. He wouldn't blame her if she spilled them now. Or his blood. He deserved it.

"You were right about the poison. It does cause certain effects on humans. They are vulnerable to it. It acts as a stimulant, to ease the mating process. You don't love me, Kira."

She turned her eyes away from him. That one motion caused the pain in his chest to worsen and spread down to his legs. He wished once again that he'd never set eyes on her. Perhaps then the pain in his chest would not feel as if it were crushing the life from him.

He had owed her an answer but what should have been simple became complicated beyond belief. She was his, his! But she was also so powerful. Kira didn't even know how she was a pawn in the game of control of Tyr. Her father, the king of Karn, controlled the largest army next to Tyr's. When the two kingdoms joined, it would be winner take all. With Kira at his side and Karn's army at his back Damon would be unstoppable.

All of that had happened so long ago, and now the woman who still lay sleeping in his arms needed an explanation. She needed to know what Mace had done to her when he found her on the eve of her wedding to Damon. He needed to tell her that he was not a man, that a beast lingered just beneath his flesh and she carried some of the beast with her. She shifted in his arms. She had told him she remembered him but there was still so much she didn't know. Her reaction to his mention of Mace was less than spectacular, making him think that she did not even recall the man who had left his mark on her skin.

Even though she had opened her body to him, there was much about her relationship with Damon that she still did not recall. He wanted to force the memories to come to her, wanted her to know how much they loved one another, but his own betrayals kept him from waking her now and telling her everything.

He had searched for her at first when she disappeared. Then he had nearly driven himself insane thinking of where she may be and why she had not returned to him. Finally he had all but given up on her. His searches of the nearby planets had yielded nothing.

He knew they were not safe here. He had to find a way to return her to Tyr, to face down Mace and to put an end to the battle for the throne. But first he had to find Tambourne and his medallion.

Chapter Six

He had to find Tambourne. Kira didn't know it, but the poison from Mace's bite had worked its way into her system and slowly bonded with her. The fact that she was here instead of on Tyr had somehow managed to slow its reaction to her body and her body's reaction to it. Now she was at the mercy of the moons just as Damon was. Their joining would last well beyond one night, beyond their time in New Orleans.

If he could find a way to return himself.

Tambourne was easy enough to find. The haggard look of the day before had been replaced with the look of a man who was well put-together, from his starched suit to his impeccable hair. Damon groaned as he eyed the man who had laid claim to his amulet.

"Tambourne. You have something of mine."

The man looked up from his drink as Damon sat across from him. He sat in the bar, just beyond where Kira was busy signing video game covers. Laying in wait, if Damon knew anything about predatory behavior.

"And you have something of mine. Perhaps we can strike a deal." The man's smile was slow and easy but there was a hint of something in his eyes Damon couldn't quite read.

"I will not strike a deal with you."

"Then you won't get what you want. An amazing little trinket, this necklace of yours. Just yesterday the need for blood, the need to change by the moon and kill, was unreal. I couldn't think. Then this necklace called out to me, demanded that I take it from her. As soon as I slipped it around my neck the drive to feed, to change, it all died down. You say you aren't like me. Then why is it that you need the amulet?"

"I need it for reasons beyond what you explain."

"No. You need it to control your devil. I can see inside your head, man. It has told me your secrets, the ones you didn't reveal to me. Kira's games. I know all about them now. I know about that mark on her neck. More than what you told me. *I know everything*." The last words were a challenge. Pack leader to pack leader. There could only be one alpha male, and Damon refused to let this man take his birthright.

"I am listening."

"I know you need to get home. I don't want to fight you. I wouldn't win. Look at us, not quite an equal match, eh?"

No, they weren't. Even though this man was large, he would not be able to hold his own against a dragon. "Go on."

"I can help you. I study things that don't exist. Like me and you."

"And?"

"And I have friends who study them, too. Friends who have discovered things they don't know how to comprehend. You get what I'm saying?"

"I am not making a deal with you. Kira is free to make her own decision."

"You and I both know that isn't true. You plan to bring her back with you, to show her the world she doesn't remember. What you didn't tell me, your little charm here did. I see the way you look at her, how you sit now in between her and me. You will protect her at all costs, but can you protect her from yourself?"

"Leave her to me."

"I plan to. She isn't what I want."

"Then what?"

"I want to see this world of yours. You tell me where it is, I help you get there, you take me with you."

Damon studied the man for a second, taking in every line of his face, every vein that pulsed beneath the surface. He was as much a prisoner here as Damon had been at home. And, like Damon, all he wanted was a means to escape. For Damon, escape came with a price.

"And what will you do in a world filled with things you can't understand?"

"Ah, but I do understand. I am one of them. I am a werewolf. Going to a world of monsters would be like going home. Finally, I would have a place to belong."

"Ours is not a world of monsters."

"Suit yourself." He leaned back in his chair and tossed back the remainder of his drink. "I know differently."

"I haven't told her the truth yet. Give me time to explain to her. Then you and I can discuss this."

"Make it quick. The full moon is in three days. I plan to keep your charm until after the full moon. Just to see if it will affect my change."

"And if it does?"

"Then that opens up a whole new world of possibility, doesn't it?"

"Perhaps so."

"Look, I'll get back to you. Let me contact my friends. In the meantime, can you give me an idea about where your world is located?"

"And why should I trust you with that knowledge?"

"Because you have no way of going home without me."

Tambourne spoke the truth. Damon had not been able to find a way home. There was no secret passage from this tiny world to his. The only connections he had to his world were the amulet and the woman who sat in the next room, completely unaware that she was alien to this planet.

"I will give you the information you need but I cannot guarantee you safe passage. Mine is a world of uncertainty. To go there would be to place yourself in danger."

"I'm already in danger."

"I need to see a map of the stars. I need to see what you see from here."

"I can do better than that. Give me an hour, and I'll have a map of the whole bloody universe."

* * * * *

The day had been long and Damon wasn't sure how much more he could take. Leland Tambourne had been true to his word. The map he produced detailed worlds most did not know existed. As a scientist of things that did not exist, as he put it, he was friends with those who studied places that did not exist. Damon's world was near the far edge of those places and was virtually unreachable from Earth. But there had to be a way. Not once but twice people had moved from his planet to this one, leaving only one conclusion. There must be a way.

Then there was Kira. Last night with her had been heaven, but today had been a chore. He had watched her move all day, weaving through the crowd, taking tiny sips of coffee, licking her lips. He had watched her jeans hug her body as she signed video game disks and covers. Her smile was radiant as she greeted each new person with the presence of an angel, sending her light to those who came into contact with her.

But all Damon wanted to do was come. The need to be inside her overruled every other need he felt. Several times today, her hand had brushed against his and all his blood emptied into his cock and his seed threatened to spill over. They had shared something magical the night before as they loved each other, something sacred and profound that he had never experienced before. He swore he was growing to love the woman he barely knew, the woman who did not remember her time with him. And the desire to tell her the truth was strong.

When he finally got her alone in their room he wasted no time moving toward her, closing in on her to claim her, to sink himself into her. He would never tire of her, never love her enough. He felt it as they crashed against the wall, her body pressing against his as she arched her back, ground her jeans-covered pussy against his leg and sent him to another level of longing.

Damon's hands fumbled with her blouse before finally tearing two of the buttons from the silk, leaving tangled threads in their place. If he didn't have his hands on her breasts soon he would die from longing. It had been hours since they last held each other and already the need for her had worked its way into his system, rendering him helpless against her scent.

She smelled like lilacs and heaven—a unique blend of woman, strength and desire. He could drown in her scent and never come up for air, which was exactly what he planned to do as soon as he pulled her jeans from her hips. She wore them tight, accenting her curves, but right now, as his hands feverishly worked, they were too tight, too restrictive, making him long for the dress she had worn the evening before, the dress that would never be worn again due to his lack of care in removing it.

He pulled her with him as he moved to the bed, hoping they landed on the soft covering and didn't fall to the floor.

"Damon," her voice was strained. Her hands rested on his shoulders, half in hesitation. He knew she still wasn't sure about him, didn't know what to make of him. But he also knew that the desire to possess her, to have all of her, was one he could not deny.

"Shh…let me love you, Kira. I have wanted to touch you all day as I watched you walk through the convention, smiling, speaking to strangers. I want you all to myself. I want you to know what you do to me."

She blushed as he spoke. That was something he loved about her, and, yes, he knew it was love. There was no other explanation for the feelings choking in his chest. He had only known her for one Earth day, a period of twenty-four hours, yet he knew deep inside that he would never allow her to leave him. She had become the woman she was before she betrayed him. His need for her grew and he knew he would protect her once they returned home. Whatever had been done there, he would undo.

"Damon, I can't..." She hesitated again, her nails digging into his shoulder as he knelt down to rid her of her jeans. Her silk shirt half hung off her frame, her lacy black bra peeking out from beneath.

"Can't what, love?"

"I never meant to..." Sobs choked her and he tried not to let them stop him. Love the tears away, his inner voice said, yet the fear in her eyes stopped him short.

"Never meant to what?" His hands rested on her waist as he paused in removing her jeans.

"I never meant to let things go this far. I have to leave in the morning and you have to get back to your life. I'm just not the one-night stand kind of girl."

"The what?"

"One-night stand. You know, have sex with a total stranger and then leave. That's not me." She bit her bottom lip after she spoke then she removed his hands and sank down onto the bed.

"Is that what you think? That I will love you and then ask you to leave? No. I will not. I will never leave your side."

"I bet you say that to all the girls." She fell backward so that he couldn't see her face, but he felt the tears as they flowed down her cheeks. They gripped his chest, causing a pain unlike any he had ever felt. A lover's tears, a true lover's tears, would do that to the one who loved her. And Damon knew he loved Kira. There was no doubt in his mind. It no longer mattered what Kira had done to him before. She was a new woman, renewed for him, given to him as a second chance at happiness. He knew he had to tell her the truth, show her the truth. But how?

"I say that to you because I love you. I want you to be with me. I want to take you home with me."

"You want to what?" She sat up, the tears still flowing. She wiped them on the back of her hand and then pulled her shirt closed around her. He inhaled sharply as her ample breasts were once again hidden from view, his frustration mounting.

"I want you to come with me, come home. I want you to be mine."

She licked her lips, looking as if she were contemplating her words. He could feel her heartbeat increase its rhythm as her hands fisted in the bed covering. Why was she so afraid of him? He knew, intrinsically, that she feared him because she had glimpsed the dragon inside him somewhere in the heat of passion. Damon knew the dragon sometimes appeared at will, taking over his features with its stark, demonic face. She knew that the man who knelt before her, baring his heart to her, was no man at all. Perhaps she even sensed their past.

"I must tell you the truth, Kira. I must show you all of me. Are you ready for that?"

"I'm not ready for any of this."

"I want to show you wonders you have only dreamed of. Your game, it is a fantasy land, no?"

"Yes. It is a fantasy land. Places like that, people like that, don't exist."

"What if I told you they do? What if I told you those things you spoke of to the room full of admirers was true? There is a world outside your own."

"You're nuts." This time, she stood and walked over to the window. She pulled the curtain back, allowing the moon to shine through. Damon longed to go to her and wrap his arms around her. Instead he stood, his eyes content to caress her back while she contemplated his announcement.

"No, Kira. I'm not nuts, as you put it. I am telling you that I can give you so much more than what you have here. I can give you a life where you will never want for anything in a place where fantasies, your fantasies, can come true."

"Well, let's go, then." When she turned to face him, he could hear the sarcasm as the words flew from her lips. "Let's go now to this fantasy world of yours. Come on, take me."

"You don't believe me."

"No, I don't. Look, Damon, you're incredibly beautiful, a wonderful lover, a kind man, but none of this is real. This thing between us is nothing but sex. You feel it, I feel it. You know it can't last, not here and not in some land you've created."

"What if I prove you wrong?"

"How would you do that?"

"I can't do it here. But if you will come with me, out into the night, I will reveal everything to you. And then you'll know I speak the truth. But, Kira, please, do not fear me."

"I'm not afraid of you," the unsteady tone of her voice was not lost on him. She was afraid of what she didn't understand. He would be, too. He had been at one time, when he didn't understand the change that ruled his kind, binding them to lovers they sometimes did not choose.

"I shall never harm you. I never want to see fear flash in your eyes. But I have a deep truth to reveal to you and you may not like it, Kira. You may never want me to touch you again, but you must. You hold my heart in your hands and you must know that I love you."

"What is it you have to show me?"

"Your past."

* * * * *

His words echoed in her head long after they left the hotel room. He had taken her out into the streets of New Orleans, a place that was both frightening and fascinating. The sounds of the night, of year-round Carnival rang in the air, sending a chill down her back as she thought of Anne Rice's vampires and the rumors of otherworldly creatures that frequented the night here.

Not many towns claimed a legendary voodoo queen or routine vampire and ghost tours. New Orleans was one of those places. Knowing this forced her to move closer to Damon as they wove in and out of the people, most of whom she recognized from the convention. Damon's big hand held firmly to hers as they moved but it didn't provide the kind of protection she needed.

Kira knew she was afraid, even if she didn't want to admit it to Damon. His secret, whatever it was, must be huge, almost as huge as the man who loomed over her. Her heart leapt into her throat as several scenarios flew through her mind at once. Maybe he was a serial killer and she his latest victim. Love 'em and kill 'em? No, that wasn't him. When she looked into his eyes she swore she could see his soul, and it was not tainted by blood. But there was something dark in there, something she couldn't readily define.

"Where are we going?"

"I'm taking you somewhere safe, somewhere I discovered my first night here. I needed a haven, time to understand things, and this place provided it."

They turned onto Ann Street and made their way past several tiny shops. Gypsies and jewelers hung out in the doorways of the shops as tourists began leaving, heading toward Bourbon. One set of dark eyes followed them as their owner crossed herself and whispered something in French. The prayer sent a chill crawling up Kira's back as she thought she heard the French word for *devil*, but couldn't be sure.

She didn't ask any more questions as they moved quietly through the night. Instead, she focused on the feel of Damon's heartbeat in her hand. He was gripping her hand so tightly, as if his very life depended on the connection. He loved her, he had said. God, could she believe him? It hurt too much to think about what she would do if those words were true.

She shook herself, trying to erase her fears. Even though she really didn't feel as if she were in danger there was still no need to let her guard down. They had been alone in her room and he had made no unwelcome moves toward her. In fact, everything he had done to this point had been so very welcome.

"We are here."

He pushed open an old door that looked as if it would fall from the hinges if it so much as moved. She clung to him as they stepped inside and were immediately assaulted by the scents of dirt and mold. He moved through the dark as if he were made for it, carefully leading her through a maze of a house.

"We're almost there."

She couldn't see a thing as they had moved beyond the windows. They seemed to now be in an endless tunnel with no way out. Her eyes couldn't focus in the darkness as he gently pulled her behind him. Fear gripped her heart as she wondered what he would do next. She bit her lip, only stopping when she tasted blood. The moment of reckoning was at hand and she was damned if she knew what to do about it.

* * * * *

The room was instantly lit, though Kira wasn't sure of the source. Damon must have lit a well-known torch on the wall or candles or something. When he turned, she saw the source, which was in fact two torches, one of which he held in his hand. Wrapping her arms around herself, she watched as he moved across the room to deposit the other torch into a bracket on the opposite wall.

This place was a haven. A low bed lay against one wall while several articles of clothing lay across an old chair. A sword hung on one wall and a fireplace invited them to sit and enjoy themselves. But there was still something menacing in the air, something hanging between them that he had yet to reveal.

"I brought you here because I do not want you to escape."

Her fingernails dug half-moons into her palms as he removed his overcoat and flung it over the back of the chair where it joined the rest of his clothing.

"Are you going to kill me?" She had to ask even though deep down she knew he wouldn't harm her.

"No. I'm not going to kill you."

"Then why did you bring me here?"

"Do you like dragons, Kira?"

"I don't understand what that has to do with anything."

"Tell me about your game, about *Dragon's Law*. What inspired it?"

"I don't know." But she did know. A series of dreams had inspired it, dreams so real they almost seemed like they were from another dimension, as if they were some forgotten part of herself.

"The amulet you had. Did you recognize it?"

"No. I didn't recognize it when I bought it. I just liked it."

"It is like the charm in your game, the one your hero wears, the one you never can quite see."

"How do you know?"

"I watched others play it at the convention. I saw how he moved, how he changed, how he held onto his mortality through his amulet. I watched your fantasy come to life and I knew then that you would understand this."

"So far, I don't understand anything."

"No, but you will. As soon as I reveal all to you, you will understand and you'll *know*. You'll know, Kira."

Tears threatened to spill out as everything he said seemed to have a double meaning. What had she gotten herself into? She didn't want to be afraid of him, didn't want to believe that anything about him could be bad.

"Tell me, then."

"If I tell you, promise you will believe me."

She nodded, though she wasn't sure she could really promise.

"I am not from here. I am from somewhere far away, a land called Tyr-LaRoche. It is a world much like yours once was, with kings and castles. But it is different, too." He sank down onto the bed as he spoke, but she refused to follow him, wanting to remain close to the doorway, not that she could find her way out if she tried.

"Go on."

"It is a land of dragons. The men there are cursed to become dragons. By the dark moon, they change, and if they do not find a lover by morning they will lose control of the dragon inside. They can fight it off, some of them. Some have talismans that help them. Others have strong will. But eventually all must mate. Mates are bound for one moon time, an Earth month. And, Kira, you are my mate."

A laugh escaped before she could stifle it. Dragons and mates? Yeah, he was crazy. "I don't believe any of this."

"The necklace you wore is my amulet. My brother, Mace, took it from me and tossed it into a vortex, an anomaly that appears only under the eclipse. It sent the necklace to you but I came as well. I threw myself into it because my amulet, the necklace around your neck, is the one thing that aids my control. Without it, I was weak. The first night we were together I needed you desperately.

"When Leland Tambourne took it from you it opened you up to the fever. Having me near you, as a reminder of home, your body reacted and you needed me, too."

His confession did not help his case. He made love to her last night because he needed sex? Never mind the dragon bit, which she didn't believe for a second. "Look, I don't know what's wrong with you, but I am sure a good psychiatrist can…"

"Kira, please don't make me show you."

"Show me what? That you're off your rocker? Come on, Damon. I've heard some lines before, and some pretty amazing stories, but dragons?"

"You believe in them."

"No, I don't," she lied. Everything inside her believed in them but how could she tell him that?

"Your game speaks differently. I have seen it. I have seen the inner workings of your mind."

"It's a game, Damon. Nothing else. Come on, it's how I make my living. You can't think that I believe…"

"Watch me, Kira. Look into my eyes."

She let out an exasperated sigh and crossed her arms. He was nuts. Abso-freaking-lutely nuts.

"What are you gonna do? Change into a dragon? Go ahead, Damon, change."

It started in his eyes. The gray glow ignited with gold and then changed to red as his eyebrows rose and seemed to melt right into his forehead. His hair, which had been long to begin with, seemed to grow, sliding down his back as his hands reached for his shirt to reveal the dark mass there. His beard also lengthened, covering his neck as if the hair were literally striving to cover his entire body.

He shed his shirt and pants as his skin changed from golden to black. She couldn't breathe as she watched the scales appear. If a scream had existed anywhere in her throat she was sure it would have erupted. It didn't. Instead, her heart stopped, her breath stopped and her eyes refused to look away.

Damon's hands, the ones that had roamed her body last night and this morning, disappeared, having been replaced by something entirely inhuman. Fingernails that had dug into the bedsheets as she had taken his cock into her mouth were now talons. And his face, God, his face! The beautiful Norse features that had defined his square jaw disappeared as his chin lengthened and the scales spread to cover his cheeks, his chin, his ears. Even his lips were covered with a fine, dark coat. Only his eyes remained slightly human, but the red glow there made them more monstrous than not.

Kira had never fainted before, had never hoped to faint, but everything inside her willed her to fall, to pretend this was a dream. If she fell maybe she would dream and would wake up still cradled in Damon's arms, none of this having happened. But she didn't faint as the dragon held her in his icy gaze, his tail swishing back and forth like a cat's.

She opened her mouth to speak but the words wouldn't come out as fear paralyzed her. And to her amazement the creature moved forward, his dragon's tongue peeking out from what had once been Damon's mouth. He bent his head forward, his nostrils flaring, as he sniffed the air for her scent. Crouched low, he let out a growl. That was all it took for Kira to find her feet again.

The only thought on her mind was getting the hell out of there. This was some kind of sick dream or nightmare or something. There were no words to describe what this was or to combat the lust in the dragon's eyes as he leapt for her, almost knocking her off balance with his nose as it hit against her.

His teeth were massive as he grinned at her, threatening to rip her flesh from her bones, and threw his head back in a chilling howl. Then he approached.

"What are you going to do to me, monster? Are you going to eat me?" She inhaled sharply as his hot breath washed over her body. Her backside made contact with the hard wall preventing her retreat from the monster, forcing her to face him down.

"You can't kill me," the words barely formed in her throat. She held her head high, attempting to appear fearless as her heart raced.

His face was but a foot from her as his eyes locked onto her. When he pounced the sheer force of being thrown to the ground almost knocked her unconscious. Before she could recover he was on top of her, one paw stretched across her lower half, holding her in place.

She wanted to crumble against the floor and give up, die gracefully, but everything in her screamed out that she should fight. If her arms would move she would pound her fists into his scaly flesh until he finished the deed, killing her if that was what he wished. But nothing was working. The only things that seemed to be functioning were her hammering heart and the tears that had not stopped.

"Kira," the voice came from deep inside the dragon and sounded like nothing more than a growl.

"Get away from me." The words finally erupted from somewhere deep in her chest, the same place the tears were now coming from.

"Kir-a," the word was barely audible from beneath the dragon's breath. It didn't endear him to her. Instead, it scared the hell out of her as she felt her knees go limp beneath her.

She would die here, like this, with the dragon looming above her, his once beautiful face now covered with a mask of scales. The mouth that had loved her so carefully, ripping her to pieces.

"Please," it was the only thing she could say as his head dipped down, his tongue lashing out to run along the leg of her jeans. There was nothing erotic, nothing desirable about the reptilian tongue as it moved against the outer edge of her shirt.

Thoughts raced through her mind, the first of which was what to do if he decided to make her the dragon's mate. She couldn't, wouldn't make love to him in this state. "Please let me go." Uncontrollable sobs tore through her body as thoughts that felt more like memories washed over her. Her shoulder ached, and she knew there had been a dragon somewhere in her past. There had been so much blood, so much pain. She heard his voice in her head, screaming her name in pain. "Kira!"

"Do not fear me," the words were hissed from his reptilian tongue and they sent a shiver down her back. His tongue flicked out and ran across her shirt, making her cringe at the movement. God, she hoped he didn't plan to rape her! How would she survive such an attack? Would she survive? She looked into his snarling face and tried to muster up the courage she needed to survive this. It was then that their eyes locked and he once again looked like the man she had danced with, the man who had sent a delightful shiver down her back with one tiny kiss.

He lightened his hold on her then dipped his head between her legs and let his tongue roam along her body. She quivered at the sensation in spite of her fear. He wasn't a dragon. He was a man, and the desire she had felt for him upon first seeing him combined with the fear from seconds ago to erupt somewhere in her chest and pool in the place where his tongue was now moving.

This wasn't right. This was so not right! Everything inside her should be protesting, raging, screaming to the top of her lungs. Instead, she lay there, her eyes locked with the dragon's eyes, suddenly no longer concerned that he would kill her. The humming that began somewhere deep inside the stone escaped and surrounded them, illuminating the tomb with a golden light. This was going to be okay. Something inside promised her that this would be okay and she would not be harmed. His dragon tongue slid across her flesh, and she was unable to fight, unwilling to fight.

"Please don't hurt me."

His head moved down to rest against hers, to nuzzle her as a pet might, but his massive front legs still rested on either side of her shoulders, holding her in place as he conveyed his affection.

"Never," she heard the human voice from beneath the dragon's skin. Then, as she lay there, helpless beneath him, the man she had known slowly reappeared, his human skin finally resting warm against hers.

She swallowed hard. What the hell was she supposed to do now?

She squeezed her eyes tightly as her hands reached out and made contact with the loose strands of his jet-black hair. Holding her with his large paws, his talons threatening to pierce her skin, he lowered his mouth to hers. The talons on her thighs melted away into fingers and his paws became human hands and his tongue became fevered as it slipped inside her mouth, which, to her surprise, had welcomed him.

He growled against her skin as the last of the beast left his body. She heard the sound of his tail hitting the dirt floor. But she was already lost in the sensation of his tongue as it moved across her mouth, probed then retreated, licked, lapped, sucked. And she wanted to die for her the way her body betrayed her, the way she wanted the man who only seconds ago she thought would kill her.

Trust him. The voice sounded like liquid gold and had no human source. The pulsating rhythm of his heart against her chest throbbed the words as she arched her back, giving him access to her innermost core as his hands slid down her body, unbuttoned her jeans and sought out her warmth.

She would trust him, she decided before she became lost in the sensation of his hands as they helped her out of her clothes and then carried her to his bed. She was lost to him, to this man, this monster. And she would go with him to this other world, wherever it may be, but first, she wanted him to take her to heaven, something he seemed intent upon doing.

When Damon entered her body they made a pact. Wordlessly. She knew she could never let him go, she felt it in the swelling of her heart, in the way her body opened for him as if she had been waiting for him all her life. She arched against him, wrapping her arms around him, dragging his mouth against hers. Her tongue shot inside his mouth, claiming him in the same way he had claimed her.

She was crazy. There was no other way to explain what was happening to her. This man who lay buried inside her body had just turned into a dragon, just proclaimed himself to be of another world and she'd accepted him. Worse, she'd let him love her, and she knew she would die without him.

"I love you, Kira," he whispered against her lips. Slowly, his cock moved in and out of her body. She looked up at him, watched his face morph from dragon to man and back again, watched the thousands of colors play in his eyes.

"Don't talk, Damon. Just love me."

His breath brushed across her face, sending shivers of delight through her as she felt her orgasm build slowly. This time, he stoked the slow-burning embers until they erupted in a blaze and threatened to ignite them both. When she lay in his arms, spent from their lovemaking, she knew things would never be the same after this night.

* * * * *

They lay in the darkness back in her hotel room, her fingers tracing tiny circles along his chest. He heard her heavy breathing, felt the sadness overtake her body just before she spoke.

"Tell me about Mace. You mentioned him before."

This again. The last thing he wished to discuss with her was his brother. "Mace is my brother."

"You obviously hate him."

"We do not get along."

"The first night of the convention, why did you say he bit me?"

"I did not think you recalled that. You were so fevered that night."

"It's a little foggy but I do remember you saying that. Why did he bite me? I don't understand." She pulled from his arms and sat up, her body barely visible to him in the darkness.

"No, I suppose you don't."

"You don't want to talk about this."

"No, I don't. I don't have all the answers you seek. Only you know why you and Mace…why he bit you."

"Why are you being like this?"

"Like what?"

"So cold to me. What did I do to make you hate me?"

He reached out to her, his chest aching with the possibility that *she* could hate *him*. "I don't hate you, Kira." *I wish to the gods I did.* "Now, let us sleep."

Sleep wouldn't come as thousands of thoughts raced through his head. One screamed out above the rest. What if she chose Mace instead of him?

Chapter Seven

Things don't always look the same in the light. That was the first thought sweeping through Kira's mind as dawn awoke her, washing over her body, illuminating the man sleeping next to her. He was a dragon, she reminded herself, remembering last night's strange revelation.

Today the outside world would invade and she would have to make a decision. Several, actually. There was the small matter of what to do about Damon now that she knew what he was and what he intended. But there was also what to do about her heart, which was filled with uncertainty.

Okay, so she had gotten what she wanted. She had the hot fling with probably the best-looking guy she had ever seen. The fact that he turned out to be a magnificent lover and the object of her every fantastic wish were both just icing. But she wasn't in love with him and really wasn't sure if a woman like herself was capable of love, especially not the kind he spouted from his sensual lips.

She gave herself a mental shake before pulling her body from beneath his arm. She needed time to think, time to sort all these emotions out and figure out exactly what she was supposed to do with the man who lay sleeping. Padding quietly to the bathroom, she opened the door and stepped inside, hoping it would provide sanctuary from the craziness swimming around in her head.

Everything in here reminded her of him. It wasn't a haven but a monument to what had happened and the things he had promised. Damon wanted to take her to another world, a place where dragons weren't myths, a place where the men were like him. She couldn't expect to just jet-set to this other planet and be treated as any sort of equal. But she knew this other planet was home. Even though she didn't have all the details yet, she knew she belonged with Damon, and she knew his world was her home.

What are you thinking? She examined the reflection she hardly recognized. The Kira who had come to New Orleans was certainly not the one standing before her, threatening to lose her freaking mind by traveling into outer space. No, there had to be another way to solve this problem that had been thrust on her.

I can't go with him. The thought struck her as she turned on the warm water and began filling the tub. There was no way she could leave. She had too much going for her here, too many responsibilities. Yet, her heart sank at the thought of being away from him. She wasn't in love with him yet, but she knew she could easily fall for the man who had captured her imagination and brought her body back to life. She swore her breasts didn't sag nearly as much as they had three days ago. And her hair had a luster that had long been lost.

Kira sank into the tub, wishing the answers would come to her, wishing she could figure out what to do about Damon and the huge hole that still rested in her chest. She started when the door opened to reveal a very naked, very aroused Damon. God, the man was gorgeous. She had never been one for facial hair but the short beard he wore only accented his rugged good looks. Then there was the commanding way he walked into a room, be it a bathroom or a ballroom. He demanded she take notice and caused a reaction deep inside her aching body, one that begged for release.

"Good morning." His voice was strained, reflecting the lack of sleep they had gotten recently.

"Good morning." She tried not to sink further into the bubbles, hiding her breasts from view, but the reaction was one that was out of habit more than anything else.

"Today is the day you must leave this place."

"Yeah, I check out of the hotel today."

"And you are coming with me."

It wasn't a question yet she saw the uncertainty flash in his eyes. It was the first time he had ever displayed any kind of emotional weakness to her and she hated to admit how her heart thumped wildly at the thought. He claimed to love her but she knew love didn't happen overnight. Not even with spacemen, which, she realized, he was.

"Damon, I don't know about this…" she started, but he quickly shut her up when he placed one of his large fingers against her lips.

"I know. I will protect you, Kira. I know you are concerned about my people and my land but you will be safe with me."

She believed him. It wasn't that she didn't, it was just that this whole situation was still so difficult to wrap her head around. A man from another world sat inches from her, his hot breath fanning across her face, his rough finger grazing her lips and all she wanted to do was melt herself into him and pretend that this was the real thing.

"It's not that." Reluctantly she pulled away from his hold. "How do you even know we can return?"

"I know. Now, no more questions."

"But…"

He stepped into the tub, forcing some of the water to run along the sides as his weight settled. "Shh…Sweet Kira."

She wanted to take him home, wanted to be what he needed. God, she wanted it so badly. Her chest ached at the thought of disappointing him but she didn't know enough about her past. Everything was still so foggy. It came back to her in her sleep, but when she was awake it was so difficult to make sense of it all. "Damon…"

"No, don't talk. I want you to love me. I want to be inside you. Do you feel me?" He moved closer to her, took her hand and placed it on his hard penis. She sucked in her breath at the same time he did.

Her fingers closed around his hard shaft as he sank closer to her, his big body knocking her off balance as she tried to slide over. She ended up falling against his chest, one hand landing there while the other began stroking him slowly. God, she loved watching his eyes glow golden when he was turned on, and she loved the way he growled low and long when he wanted her.

He leaned against her, his head touching hers. The only thing she could concentrate on was the way his cock felt in her hand and the way his body rocked against her as she stroked him.

Her fingers seemed to know his body as well as they knew her own. She knew how to move along his shaft, how to make the fire in his eyes increase. Never having been confident in her sexual ability, Kira loved the freedom he gave her, the way he made her feel as if she could do no wrong. She became bold with him, willing to try things she had never even considered in the past. Now, she licked her lips, knowing exactly what she wanted to do to him.

"Stay still," she warned as she moved over him, keeping his cock in her hand. Slowly, she raised herself out of the tub, just long enough to grab her waterproof lubricant and bring it with her into the tub. All it took was a little drop to rub along her labia and inside her vagina.

He gave a slow smile as he watched her move. Her reflection watched her eyes smolder over with lust as she lowered herself onto him, boldly doing that which she had never done before. His cock remained perfectly still, his back rigid as she moved slowly, taking him into her body inch by glorious inch. Finally she sat against him, his cock firmly planted inside her, his head rolled back against the mirrored wall behind the tub.

Insecurity swept through her for a second, until she heard his low growl and knew she had pleased him. She raised herself up, forcing his cock to move out of her body. Then, slowly, slowly, she lowered herself again. Her clit rubbed against his rough pubic hair as she moved, sending a wave of fire through her body. Again, she raised herself up and then took him into her.

Freedom. This was what Damon did to her, he gave her to freedom to explore her needs and desires and to take control. Bracing herself by placing her hands on his shoulders, she began rocking back and forth and then moving up and down again. Rather than watching his reaction she was lost in her own through the mist rising from the tub and Damon's heat. Her cheeks were reddened, her eyes glazed with want. This woman who was making love to Damon was radiant! She was not the frumpy Kira who had come to the convention at all.

And this Kira was lost in watching the ecstasy as it washed over her, as she threw her head back in release. Her orgasm built deep inside her womb, starting a web of tremors, one after the other. Her nails bit into his shoulders as she quaked around him, moaning, calling out his name and placing kisses on his jaw.

Finally, he gripped her hips, holding her still as he moved within her. She was so lost in the orgasm she couldn't raise herself off him, couldn't force her pussy to release him. He took control, raising her and then placing her back down until he filled her completely. Her arms hung limply around his shoulders as he growled again, his cock straightening even more inside her as he shot his hot seed into her womb.

Sweat dripped down his chest and her face as their hair matted together. Their breaths came in slow bursts, each spent in the other.

When he ran his hand along her spine, she shivered against him, not from cold, but from longing. God, she wanted to be everything he needed. But to go home with him may require more than she could manage. Still, she was willing to give it a try.

As sleep descended upon her, she knew everything he had told her had been the truth. She was from another place and Damon was part of her soul. She need him now just as she had before, even as she felt that need had been her downfall.

Need. It was all about need. And, God, how she needed him.

Sleep took over once more, enveloping her in the familiar haze of a planet she couldn't recall during her waking hours. She and Damon had spent precious moments together there, and now, she knew her body longed to return home to the man she loved. But so much stood between them. There was a past she couldn't fully understand, mistakes she felt guilty for making but could not recall. Then there was the pain in her heart as she wondered whether or not Damon could ever love her.

She remembered a night so long ago. They had been together for two weeks when she realized she would not be able to control the rage inside his body. The night came back to her as clearly as if it were yesterday.

She sat just at the edge of the line of trees, watching him. His wild hair blew in the nightly wind, his stance was fit for a king. He would make a wonderful ruler someday. And he would probably have by his side a woman whom he both needed and loved, someone who was not leverage against his brother.

Drying her tears on the back of her hand, Kira waited until the sky darkened further, unwilling to allow him to see the pain on her face. She would go to him tonight, if only to help him keep his strength, but she would erase all thoughts of love from her mind as she spread her legs for him, allowed him to invade her body, to take from her the nectar he needed to survive.

"You have returned." His brows were tightly knit as he gazed down at her.

"Yes. It is late."

"Perhaps we should retire then." He stepped aside, allowing her to pass and enter the cavern before him. She watched as he rolled a large boulder into place at the opening, leaving enough room for fresh air to enter yet closing out all invading forces.

She bit her lip, wondering how he would take her tonight. Would he be soft and gentle or was he already tiring of her? Perhaps he would simply go through the motions, stoking her fire only enough to enter her and spill his seed before he pulled out, leaving her filled with his hot juices and empty of all else.

He busied himself with setting up their bed, a makeshift roll of soft fabric that would provide sufficient protection against the hard dirt floor. She watched as the shadows from the fire illuminated his face, making him look as fierce as he had the night she first met him. If only she could recapture that night and her innocence! If only she could have escaped without giving her soul to him!

"Come to me, Kira," he whispered as he reclined onto the pallet.

She moved slowly, wondering if his eyes held a spark of anything other than lust. The fire played tricks on her mind, not allowing her to see his eyes as they actually were without a hint of shadow play in them.

He moved to the side as she approached, leaving room for her to lie next to him. His chest was bare and he had taken his boots off. The expanse of bare skin made her want nothing more than to run her hands along his taut muscles, feel the strength he held in them, tease his body with wild abandon. Instead, she lay next to him, willing her hands not to reach out and touch him.

"You are beautiful." He reached out to stroke her cheek, rendering her defenseless with his words and actions.

"Don't." She tried to pull away from him but was held spellbound by his magnificent eyes.

"Don't what? Touch you?"

"Don't be nice to me. You don't have to. You can just take me if you want. I won't fight you."

His hand moved and the look that colored his face made her almost wish she hadn't spoken. The dragon's face seemed to be twisted in surprise and pain. "Is that what you think? That I will simply take you for the purpose of taking?"

"No. You will take me for the purpose of survival." She held her chin high, but she wished she could look away from him. Her words only seemed to hurt him more, causing the eyes that had smoldered with desire to now mask themselves from her.

"Yes, survival. I had forgotten." His voice was low and his hand lay between them now. She would much rather have it on her face, her body. He rolled onto his back. "Sleep now."

Sleep? Her heart pounded wildly. How could he not take her? She swallowed hard, wanting to reach out to him, demand that he make love to her. When he turned his back to her, her heart sank and the pain she only thought she knew earlier magnified. She would die now, right here in this cave with the man she loved refusing to touch her, refusing to allay any of the pain she felt.

Sobs threatened to ravage her body. She held them at bay, refusing to give in, refusing to take his pity, which she knew he would give to her. The only thing she could do was turn and focus on the fire, not the man who had built it. Listening for his breathing to steady, she lay awake, wondering what to do now. He had refused her tonight, and surely this refusal would weaken him. Worse, it weakened her in a way she couldn't begin to explain.

Chapter Eight

"I need to know more about you, more about where you came from. More about home. I dream about you at night, about us. Last night, I…we…we were together in some cave. I can't remember it all, Damon, and I need those memories. I need to know what happened."

Kira lay in Damon's arms, her breath washing over his chest. He had been at her home for a week, and they planned to meet Tambourne at a place called Denver in two more days. Somehow, going home did not have the same appeal today as it had when this journey began. His amulet once more rested against his chest, having been returned to him by Tambourne, who was becoming an ally rather than a foe.

He swallowed hard. Part of her, he knew, refused to believe she was connected to him.

"What would you like to know?" They had gone over this a hundred times, so it seemed to him. Each time revealed nothing new that he had not already told her, nothing she did not already know deep down inside. Still, he took a deep breath, wondering what he could tell her to make her understand where he was from and why he needed to go back. And why he needed her.

"Please, Damon. You have to tell me about your brother."

Mace. This was one subject he always wished to avoid. He and Mace were brothers in blood but no other way were they kin. Barely civil to one another, their lives had been one long battle, each vying for his own recognition. Mace knew he was not the oldest son, yet he longed for the title, while Damon knew his illegitimacy afforded him his father's curse but not his name. The battle was one that could not be won by either of them.

Until now. The legends in his land spoke of a woman who could bring peace. Deep inside his soul, he knew Kira was that woman. This was part of the reason why he had taken her from her home so long ago, stealing her in the night like a common thief rather than a bridegroom. It was the reason why he sought her out all these years, why he vowed vengeance on Mace. Her tie to his land was far beyond mere fancy or coincidence, as she claimed. She was part of his soul. The only problem was, if she ever returned with him to Tyr, Mace had a claim to her.

Even now as she lay in his arms, both of them fresh from making love, the dragon still threatened to overpower him.

"Mace is a dangerous man."

"So you say, but I want to know why you fight."

He had already told her in the past. Long nights of lovemaking and soul-searching had revealed to her almost everything about his family and his past. "You know about Mace."

"Why do you think he tossed the amulet into the vortex? How do you think he found the vortex in the first place?"

"As I said before, the moons had eclipsed."

"And?" she prodded as her fingernails traced a circle around his nipple, causing it to tighten beneath her whisper of a touch.

"And I can't think while you're doing that." He gritted his teeth.

"Sorry." Her hand stilled against his chest. He took it into his and placed a kiss on her knuckles. She rewarded him with a lazy smile.

"You did not have to stop."

"I want you to be able to think."

"As I said, there was an eclipse, and…"

"What happens under the eclipse?"

"The sky darkens. And a vortex appears. I think this is how you got here. I believe Mace forced you somehow. Somehow he convinced you or made you come to Earth without me. I had to find you. There were so many reasons, are so many reasons. Don't you see? Life without you was killing me."

Tears streaked down her face at his confession. She sat up as his hand reached out to graze against her cheek, pushing the covers from her body, and then slid from the comforting position he'd held her in. "I can almost see it, Damon. I can see myself standing before it. The sky does darken, and the vortex does appear. And I loved you so much."

His hand shook at her confession. Was she finally remembering? "Do you remember?"

"Yes… Sort of. I can see it like it's a movie."

"That it took place twice in six years is not incredible. No one knows how often the vortex appears. Sometimes, an eclipse takes place and there is no change. Other times, the air seems to part and blackness takes its place."

"And no one knows what causes this?"

"There are no records, only legends."

"Not a very civilized people then, are you?" she teased.

"I suppose not."

"And this vortex was created where?"

"Outside the village of Waydon, the place where we get our human mates."

"Shit."

"What is it?"

"I don't know. I just can't take all of this at once. You searched for me? I mean, you really searched. You needed me that badly?"

"Yes. I still need you."

"We have to find our way home. I'm going to help you get back home, and I'm going to go with you. Damon, I know there are things in our past that I haven't figured out yet, things I can't explain. But if you trust me, if you need me as you say you do, let me try."

Tears glittered in her eyes as she spoke, making his chest ache. It hurt her to face the past, this he could clearly see. There was so much pain, so much betrayal in their past. Now, it was time to start anew. Time to start with confessions and forgiveness.

"No, Kira, don't cry. I am sorry. I took you from your home. I stole you in the night. You were there at your father's house on Tyr and I took you, bringing you in to this madness."

"Why, Damon? Why did you take me? Who am I to you?"

"You are Kira, daughter of Rudolf, King of Karn, Tyr's closest and most powerful neighbor. Whoever marries you will rule Tyr."

"So you took me to secure your throne?"

"Yes. But there is so much more. I saw you once at your father's palace. You probably don't remember. Our eyes connected for a second, and I swore I was looking into my own soul. I knew then that I must protect you from Mace. Mace wanted the throne, too. He still wishes to have it. If he found you first, if he married you… Do you understand? I couldn't allow that to happen. I knew that I needed you, and that I had to have you for my own."

"So you took me to protect me."

"In a manner of speaking. I also took you because I could not live without you."

"So betrayal runs deep for you, too."

"Yes, I suppose it does."

"But why did you take me? I remember in my dreams. I remember you telling me that you and I were bound to each other. Were we to be wed?"

"Yes. I took you because I needed to know you. And I wanted you to come to love me without being forced to."

"You did a fine job with that."

"I was wrong. And I need your forgiveness."

"It's coming back to me now. Slowly. I know your brother. I can see him standing before me, his wicked smile. He has red hair, right? Fiery hair."

"Yes."

"Mace convinced me that you would not remain faithful to me. He told me of your betrayal and told you wished for a woman with dragon's blood. That's the reason I let him bite me."

"The bite marked you as his."

"I was not Mace's lover. I know it deep down in my soul. I remember the pact he and I made. His bite would infect me with the balm, but I never knew it would mark me as his."

"But are you mine? If we return, will you be mine?"

"I have always been yours."

"You do not recall about the dragons, about our bodies, our blood, our laws?"

"Damon, it's all still so foggy. Some of it is clear as yesterday, but other parts, I can only guess at."

"The dragon's tail holds an aphrodisiac, one that is powerful enough to make you forget your inhibitions. But the dragon's bite causes his spirit, his essence to mingle with yours and you become one with him."

"Would your bite counteract Mace's?"

"I do not know. It isn't allowed."

"Well, we aren't on Tyr. We're here, on Earth. On a place where the laws of Tyr don't seem to apply. Why don't you try it and see?"

"Tambourne says you are in danger, that your body is changing due to the bite."

"Why would it change so many years later?"

"My guess is that I changed it. When I came through the portal, it caused your body to react to energy from home."

"Then you can change it again. Do it, Damon. Make me yours."

"You are mine."

"Then prove it to me."

He pulled her flush against him, his head and heart locked in a fierce battle. Turning her neck to him, she waited for his bite, waited for his poison. If he bit her, his blood and Mace's blood would mix, causing both essences to reside inside her. He knew that he must bite her. If they returned to Tyr, he would need proof of his claim to her.

Slowly, he brought his lips to her flesh, then sank his dragon fangs into her body. She clung to him and for a second he could read her thoughts as her blood spilled into his mouth and his body drank in her essence. She was afraid of him, but she loved him. Her fear tugged at his heart. She was afraid to lose him again. And he was terrified of losing her.

Licking at her wound, he closed it as soon as he was sure his spirit entered her body. They were one now. They lay wordlessly in one another's arms, not thinking. And Damon was afraid to contemplate the consequences of his actions.

* * * * *

She was not a woman without a past. She was a woman who had a past, a colorful past, and a past with this man. Staring at him, not sure if she should believe him or not, she sat on her bed, memorizing every line of his face.

There was no denying that she had fallen in love with Damon, but was it real love? Was it the kind that could make a man remain faithful and be hers forever? Did that kind even exist? In spite of her wonderful hot fling that hadn't ended yet, she wondered if what they had could be more than that.

"Tell me what you did after I left. After I found my way here?" She needed to know. Did he search for her? Did he curse her name?

"I searched for you once my anger subsided."

"Yet you did not marry. I have sisters. Surely one of them…"

"Karina. She wished to fulfill your obligation to me."

"And you refused her?"

"Yes. I did not wish to marry another."

"Even in your anger?"

"I loved you, Kira. I love you now. No one else could take your place in my heart."

"When we return, we must go to Karn, to set things right. You shall have your army."

"I no longer need an army. All I need is you."

"But if you wish for the throne…"

"I wish to have you, Kira. Now, I wish to have your heart."

"I give it willingly."

"Come to me, Kira, and love me. I don't wish to be without you again. I have fallen in love with you. I want you to know that. I have forgiven who you were and what you may have done. All I know is you, and I want you to know me."

"I love you, too, Damon. And I won't let anything stand in our way."

Chapter Nine

Denver wasn't exactly what Damon thought it would be. The bustling city their airplane landed in was quickly replaced by a mountainous countryside and snow-covered hills. Leland drove in silence, as he had been since he picked them up at the airport. He hadn't yet told Damon what was on his mind but he had a feeling it had to do with the trip back to Tyr.

Kira lay asleep on his lap in the backseat and Damon couldn't help but the feeling of fear that crept into his heart. Everything inside him knew he was placing them all in danger by opening up their world like this. Giving Leland the map to his part of the universe could be a deadly thing if he used it incorrectly.

"Are you ready for this?" Leland glanced up in the rearview mirror.

"Yes. I have been gone too long."

"I have made a decision. I don't think I'll return with you."

"Oh? Why the sudden change?"

"We've been studying this world of yours the past few days. You say it is a land riddled with warfare. Perhaps I should take my chances on familiar grounds and remain on Earth."

"What about your need to be with others like yourself?"

"It turns out that there are more like me out there. My friends and I…we had not met face-to-face before. Meeting them opened up whole new possibilities to me. Many of them are changelings, too. They change with the moon, with the tides, with various natural occurrences. It leads me to think I should stay and find out what I am before I inflict myself upon another planet."

"I respect your decision."

"I would ask you something, though. Your amulet. I know it belongs to your family. I know it is your connection to your world. But…"

"But you have found need of it as well?" Damon could see his smile in the mirror.

"Yes."

"It belonged to my father and his before him. It is necessary to control the change, to fight down the demons. I cannot part with it."

"You owe me for sending you home."

"That I do, but the amulet is not up for discussion."

They sat in silence again.

"What will you do about Kira?"

"What do you mean?" The man's question caught him off-guard.

"I mean when you get back home, do you plan to marry her?"

"What does it matter to you?"

"I am not your enemy, Damon. I have acted badly in the past, but I am here to make amends. I am helping you get home. But I want to know that she'll be safe."

"I need her."

But his heart ached at the possibility. Up until now, all he wanted was to return her and marry her, make her his forever. Now, he wasn't sure if he should pursue that line of thinking or if he should allow her to reacquaint herself with her world first.

"She is a strong-willed woman. She often mentioned your name in her dreams."

"Did she?"

"Yes. You are the reason for her games, the reason she became so obsessed with that world. I think her mind is made up. She will marry you if you ask."

"But I wonder if asking will be too much."

"Only you know that."

True. He was the only one who could decide.

"We're here."

The car came to a stop. Damon nudged Kira awake. She lazily sat up and smiled at him. "We've made it."

"Home?"

"No. To the mountains."

"Oh."

Leland stepped out of the car first and then led them to a cave cut in the side of the mountain. There was no technology, nothing Damon expected.

"This is our portal home?"

"Yes. Legends say this cave holds the key. You should step inside with your hands joined. It is a portal, and it will take you where you need to go."

"How can you be so sure?"

"Research. There was a time when our worlds were linked. Almost every civilization has dragons in its mythology. This isn't a coincidence. There was a time when your kind roamed our world freely, but it has been forgotten and passed off as legend." Leland shrugged, "Besides, if it doesn't work, you just come back out."

Damon squeezed Kira's hand before releasing it and moving to stand before Leland. "Thank you for bringing us here. I owe you. If you have need of me, if this portal works, you know you will be able to find us."

"Always."

"Are you ready, Kira?" He turned to Kira and took her hand once more.

"I'm ready."

They joined hands and stepped into the cave. They had only taken three steps in before they were greeted by a bright light and then the sensation of flight. Closing his eyes, Damon awaited the trip home with trepidation. If he lost Kira, he didn't know what he would do.

When the spinning finally stopped, he opened his eyes. They stood in a cave that looked very much like the one on Earth. The only difference was the purple glow from the cavern walls indicating a high concentration of *lerium*, a mineral only found on Tyr.

"We made it." He smiled.

"We're home?"

"I think so."

Stepping out into the light, they were greeted with the wilds of Tyr. They had, in fact, made it home. Damon's first order of business, he knew, must be to return Kira to her father. Then they would work everything else out.

"I have to take you home."

"Why? I thought we were going to go take back your throne."

"I can't do it yet. I have to return you to your father first."

"But…"

"Shh. It's the only way, Kira." He sank his hand into her hair as he pulled her to him. "Trust me. All will be well."

* * * * *

"Where is Karn?" Kira didn't stop to look back as she walked and talked, trying to focus on the treacherous mountain road ahead rather than the man behind her.

"Beyond the North Pass." His voice echoed all the way up to where she stood, setting her nerves on edge.

She continued her climb, counting three steps before she spoke again. "And when will we make camp?"

"At nightfall."

"We shall stop ahead. There is a series of caverns that will provide shelter," Damon said.

She had grown accustomed to the silence and hearing his voice caught her off-guard. It was low and strained, as if he had also been wrestling with inner turmoil today. But he hadn't. His only focus had been on Mace. Defeating Mace, keeping her from Mace, everything was about Mace.

"As you wish," she found herself forcing the words from her throat.

"We shall be safe there," he continued. "As we move ahead, we should gather wood for fire. Once we are settled in, I will find food for us."

Chapter Ten

Kira's heart hammered in her chest as they approached the palace. This was her father's home, a far cry from her little house back on Earth. All the memories she had of this place came rushing back to her and now she faced the palace with renewed strength. She remembered him taking her from her bedroom and showing her the ways of love in the cavern. And she remembered Mace and the betrayal that caused her to disappear for so long. Mace had tricked her into thinking that his bite was the only way she could keep Damon. She had been a fool then. Now, as she and Damon stood before the gates, awaiting the guards, she vowed never to betray him again.

"Prince Damon," the first one spoke, giving a little bow as he moved to open the gate.

Kira had never realized how much this place looked like a medieval fortress. They stepped forward as the gate slowly opened.

"I have come to hold audience with King Rudolf. This is Kira, his daughter."

The stunned looks on the guards' faces were quickly erased as they bowed before her. "Certainly. At once."

No one remembered her. That was the first thought that ran through her mind. Of course, she didn't exactly know these men, either. It had been six years since she had set foot on this land. They had barely made it to the door when it opened and a young woman stepped outside.

At first, Kira didn't know the girl. The lines on her face were tight and spoke of worry as well as something else she couldn't readily define. Her empty eyes met Kira's and her mouth turned up in a slight smile.

"Well, the prodigal daughter has returned. Have you no kiss for your sister?"

Karina. The years had not been kind to her. Her long, dark hair had lost its shine and Kira couldn't help but feel sorry for her, thinking she was the source of her sister's angst.

"Of course." She met Karina's smile and stepped into her open arms.

"And Damon. Do you have a kiss for me?" She stepped away from Kira and moved toward Damon.

"I am here to see your father."

"As always. You were declared dead, you know," she shot over her shoulder. Kira swallowed hard at the announcement. Declared dead. But she wasn't.

"She is here now, and prepared to honor all of her duties."

"That is nice to know. You've been gone a while yourself. Things have changed."

Kira watched as Karina pulled Damon to her. He quickly pushed away, holding her at arm's length.

"I am here to set things right," he announced.

"Sometimes even good intentions fail. You have a few promises to keep as well."

"I must speak to your father."

"And you shall. And I'll take care of my dear sister. We have so much catching up to do." Karina's hand wrapped around Kira's upper arm as she led her into the palace. "I'm sure you know the way to the study," she called back to Damon.

"Where are we going? I would like to speak to Father."

"Nonsense. Look at yourself. You look as if you've been swept up by the winds. I am sure there will be a feast tonight in your honor. It's best for you to prepare for it."

"I can look after myself, dear Karina."

There was something about Karina that bothered her, something sitting somewhere in the back of her mind. Her gut protested being alone with her sister. Even though she couldn't quite put her finger on the reasoning she knew she must be on alert.

"I am certain you can. But first, you must tell me about your amazing adventure."

Karina led her into one of the bathing rooms. Kira inhaled the scents of home as they surrounded her. There was something else in the air, too, something that told her things weren't what they seemed.

"There is nothing to tell."

"I'm sure there is. Will you eat?" Karina produced a plate of fruit from a nearby table. "Eat this and tell me all about it."

"I'm not hungry."

"It will be a while before you eat again. I would if I were you. You know Father. He'll want to see you soon. But first, you should be presentable."

Cautiously, Kira took a piece of the fruit into her hand and bit into its flesh. A satisfied smile crossed Karina's face, almost making its way to her eyes. For a second, Kira remembered those same eyes looking down at her after her encounter with Mace. The fleeting memory did not stick in her head. Nothing seemed to stick as she glanced around the room, which had started to spin.

"There's a good girl. Come into the bath. Let my men take care of you." The voice seemed to come from somewhere far away.

"You did this to me. You are the reason I was gone for so long."

Again Kira felt at the mercy of forces she couldn't explain. It was almost like she was back in the hotel with Damon that first night, feeling the fever work its way into her body, feeling the need course through her.

"Are you a dragon now, Kira? Do you feel their needs?"

"I don't know what you're talking about."

She clung to a nearby table before stumbling to the floor. Her knees scraped against the marble tile.

"You have dragon's blood in you. I was there when he bit you. I saw Mace lay claim to you. You are his now, whether you want to believe it or not. And Damon will be mine."

"No," she managed as the room began to spin.

"Yes. Tell me, dear sister, do you know what happens to a dragon's mate when she mates with another? The seed he has spilled into you causes your body to treat other men as enemies. Your body reacts to the seed and shuts down. All it takes is one man coming inside you and your body will react to protect you. But what it will do is kill you. Do you understand?"

"Get away from me…" she managed. It was no use. Too many things were swirling around in her head. There was something in that fruit, something that caused her dragon blood to heat. The desire to have sex was stronger than ever. It was something she couldn't deny.

Her pussy clenched as the blood rushed to her labia and forced her clit to swell. Her nipples hardened and her heartbeat became wild and erratic.

"That should do it, love," Karina's laughing voice made its way into her system. "All you need now is a willing mate. And when Damon finds you here with them, he shall be mine. And your title will come with him."

"No," she moaned as she felt herself being lifted into strong arms and resting against a hard chest.

"Yes. Have a good time. Damon will be here soon."

A pool sat in the center of the room and the only light came from a series of torches along the walls. Soft music played in the background and she heard whispers and giggles.

"Your needs will be met here," the man said, giving no indication of his meaning. "I shall leave you now and the attendants will be in shortly."

A sound from behind her caught her attention. Four men entered and her breath caught in her throat. They were all massive, each more beautiful than the last. The first had long golden hair and skin that appeared to have been kissed by the gods. The next was even larger with long, dark hair. The third was bald, a tribal tattoo covering the top of his head. The last had short, dark hair and eyes that were so green she could see them from across the room. All were naked to the waist, their broad chests and powerful thighs exposed. She bit her bottom lip in contemplation. What was she supposed to do with them?

"My lady." The bald one bowed and moved forward. "We are here to attend to your every need."

"Get me out of here."

"You shall leave this evening. When the banquet begins. Until then, we must prepare you. Come. Eat. Let us bathe you. You must be prepared."

"Undress now," the blond one said.

"No."

"How shall we bathe you if you are clothed?"

"It is our duty. You would dishonor us if you do not allow us to perform."

"You do not wish to dishonor us, do you?" the bald one asked, his breath close to her face.

"No," she managed.

"Then allow me to undress you," the one with the shorter hair said.

There were no words of protest in her throat, even though her head screamed out. She couldn't form a plea or a denial as her body readied itself to mate. The dragon blood coursing through her veins was stronger than the best of her intentions. The fog surrounding her forced her forward as the man placed her at the edge of the pool.

The bald one smiled. All four of them entered the water, waiting for her to follow suit. The men parted, directing her toward a set of steps at the opposite end. She walked through the water, aware of their eyes on her every movement. And aware of the strange sensation in her head that made her feel off balance and a little out of control.

Sitting on the edge of the steps, she inhaled sharply as they moved toward her, circling her, leaving her no room for escape. But something inside her refused to even consider escape. Her brain felt foggy and her body ached with longing, reminding her of the spell Damon had cast over her their first night together. Just as then, she was defenseless against these men.

"Let us please you," the short-haired man whispered, his breath coating her shoulder, sending a shiver down her back.

"What is in the fruit?" she demanded with what she could find of her voice.

"A relaxant. It will curb your inhibitions. Everyone in Karn eats the fruit. Everyone seeks their pleasure. It is the way of things," the one with long, dark hair said.

"What is your name?" Kira asked him.

"I am Rhode. This is Klaud." He pointed to the bald one. "This is Dael and the one with golden hair, the pretty boy," he laughed, "is Luc."

"I am Kira."

"We know your name," Luc smiled. "You brought the dragon king here. Tonight there will be a feast in your honor. But we must first prepare you else you will tire early and not enjoy the festivities."

She leaned her head back, as it suddenly felt heavy. It fell against Dael's shoulder as he encircled her waist with his thighs.

Luc began working the ties on her bodice, exposing her breasts as his hands moved quickly and gently. Her arms felt limp as they were raised, freeing her of her last restraints. Her breasts spilled forward and were quickly covered by large hands that began massaging her nipples. Dael's fingers began working at her neck, gently rubbing circles there to ease her tension.

She was only vaguely aware of Klaud ducking beneath the water. When his hands made contact with her thighs, she was startled for a second. Soon, he freed her legs, exposing her sex, which suddenly throbbed with longing.

"We shall wash you first," one of them said. "Then we shall play."

The words seemed to come from somewhere far away. All she could think of was the longing, the need between her thighs. Her breasts felt heavy when Luc released them. Soon, three sets of hands were on her, soaping her, rubbing her as Dael's hands continued to rub her shoulders. She felt his erection press against her bare bottom when he shifted her into his lap. The pressure of it pressed against her almost drove her mad with desire. All she wanted to do right now was turn to face him and ride him as she had ridden Damon the night before.

Damon. The name seemed to come from nowhere. How could she have forgotten about him? She had to think, had to regain control. "Lie back," Dael directed as he moved away from her, dipping her hair into the water. When she obeyed, her bottom rose out of the pool, only to be captured by Rhode's big hands. As Dael washed her hair, Rhode ran his fingers along her thighs, her stomach. She felt as if she were a bow, ready to be plucked, played.

The warm water flowed over her hair, Dael's hands working out the knots and dirt. She felt herself being lifted from the water but her body again did not feel like it belonged to her. The next sensation was one of being wrapped in warmth. The hands worked quickly to dry her after they placed her onto a high table at the back of the room.

"Now, relax, Kira. Let us serve you."

She lay spread-eagle on the table, her arms limp at her sides, unable and unwilling to protest as the men began rubbing warm oil on her body. Rhode was at her head now, drying her hair and combing it. Luc took one leg while Dael took the other. Klaud rubbed the oil into her breasts, concentrating on the nipples, tweaking them with his fingers and driving her mad with desire.

Dael's fingers worked their way up to her stomach and then down lower to cover her mound. He parted her lips, holding them open while another set of hands, Luc's, began rubbing the oil into her lips and over her clit, which was painfully swollen and begging for release. His fingers lingered just on the edge of her opening, threatening to spill inside, but the release did not come.

Too soon, she was turned onto her stomach and the games began anew, this time with the concentration on rubbing her opening from behind. Skilled fingers rubbed the edge of her anus while another set continued to work her nether lips. Her clit lay pressed against the table, throbbing, longing to be touched, teased, sucked.

Klaud's hands were no longer on her breasts, having found their focus near her shoulders.

"This one is very responsive," Luc remarked.

"Yes, she is. She would be heavenly to take." Dael's voice seemed to come from right above her pussy, as his breath brushed against her.

"You know we can't keep her. We have our orders."

"But we can still watch her come. The dragon will never know how we destroyed her. Besides, Karina is treating him to the same. You know that now he lies beneath her while she fucks herself silly on his cock."

"Perhaps we should ask the woman."

"Kira," Dael's voice was against her ear now.

"Mmmm?"

"What would you like? Do you want to be filled? Do you want us to take you?"

"Mmmmm." She couldn't find the words. The drugs in her system were too strong, stealing her voice, forcing confusion upon her.

"Is that a yes, love?"

"Mmmm. Yes."

"Say it."

"Yes. Take me." The words were barely out when she felt a cock press against her opening. Her walls spasmed in anticipation. "Damon," she managed, imagining that her lover was positioned behind her.

A growl erupted from somewhere far off and the release she sought did not come. The hands that had covered her were no longer there and she felt cold suddenly. Then she was lifted, her head resting against a hard shoulder. Damon. He was here.

"Kira, did they harm you?" his voice was strained, his breathing ragged.

"Damon," the word was barely audible even to herself. Where had he come from and how had he managed to find her?

* * * * *

Damon's heart raced as he looked down at Kira. Never had he imagined that her sister, Karina, would go to such lengths to control him. She had made it clear more than once that she planned to take Kira's place as Damon's bride and though her father had not yet signed the decree, Damon knew the man wished the same thing. But Kira was back now. She was home and she was the rightful heir to the throne, and his rightful bride. But she was also in more danger than he had thought.

Now, she had almost been destroyed. There was something that changed inside her, something to do with the curse that he did not understand. When a dragon spilled his seed during the lunar period, the woman changed, bonding with him, and if her soul, like Kira's, was already part of him, the bond was even stronger. This placed her in danger if another man chose to take her as his own. He could have lost her forever!

Cradling her in his arms, he carried her back to the chamber that had been prepared for him. The men, the fools, who had loved her, would not love again anytime soon, having been bloodied from their battle with him. Karina's minions, no less. Men who were as enslaved by pleasures of the flesh as the woman who controlled them was.

Kira still slept when he laid her on his bed. He took in a long, slow breath. Her life had been put in danger because he sought to end the battle with his brother and in doing so placed his trust in her family. He watched her sleep and vowed to protect her and his kingdom. Slowly, he reached out to her and gently shook her. They must return to his palace. But first, they must marry. Here, in front of the watchful eyes of King Rudolf and all of Karn. And Karina must pay for her continued betrayal.

His brother would know what to do. Not Mace, but Kore, one of the twins, born to his father and yet another of his lovers. Kore, like it or not, was head of security under the standing regiment that still awaited a king. Though he was not fond of military leadership, he and his other brother, Trader, both knew they must keep order until the king was chosen. Neither of them wanted the responsibility.

Now, he knew he must send word to Kore that he had returned home, and that he and Kira were to be married. A truce must be formed with Mace, also. Damon knew now that he had risked too much and would not lose Kira, no matter the cost.

"I am so sorry." He pulled her to him. Nothing would ever come between them again. He swore it.

* * * * *

It took two days for Kira to stir, thanks to the shock from drops of semen that had entered her body. For those two days, Damon remained at her side, watching and waiting while he and Rudolf, along with Kore, who had arrived the prior evening, worked on a plan to unite Tyr.

Kore was filled with knowledge about Mace and even suggested that Mace may be ready for peace as well.

"He has found a woman who loves him. He is a new man," Kore declared.

This was something Damon had to see to believe. As soon as Kira had recovered, he planned to marry her and then travel to Tyr in order to meet with Mace and his woman, Eleanora.

Karina was under arrest, being guarded by Kore, who seemed more than eager to take the job.

When Kira finally awoke, Damon's relief was immense.

* * * * *

"Damon?" Kira tried to sit up, but her head still felt foggy from her ordeal. Everything had gone wrong. She couldn't quite remember what had happened but she knew that she had come close to losing everything.

"I'm here, love."

"Where are we?" For a second, she thought she was still in New Orleans, or in her own bed at home.

"We are safe. Your father wishes to see you as soon as you are well."

"And Karina?"

"You are safe from her. You are safe from everything. You and I will be married soon."

"Mmmm. That sounds good."

"Yes, it does."

"You are everything I want, Kira."

She looked up at him, unshed tears stinging her eyes.

"Prove it to me."

"I shall prove it to you tonight. In front of all of Karn. If you will be my bride."

"I think I can manage that."

"Good. All is ready. Then it will just be you and I."

* * * * *

Her wedding day. Kira never imagined it would come or that it would come under such awkward circumstances.

Her sister had been arrested and sent to the gods only knew where. Damon's brother, Mace, was apparently ready to call a truce and had even sent a wedding present. And her father seemed overjoyed to have his daughter back even if he knew she must marry Damon within a few days.

She loved Damon, though, and knew that she needed him. Her heart would not beat without him by her side. They had gone through so much to be together, and now all those dreams she had while she was sleeping, before she had realized she was in a foreign land, they were all about to come true.

Looking across the room at Damon, she smiled. This was all going to work out. She felt it somewhere deep down in her soul. They would be able to bring a new peace to their world.

"Do you promise to always love and trust one another?" the priest asked when they joined hands.

"Yes," they both said.

"And do you promise to lead your people to your best ability, joining your two lands in a promise of peace?"

"Yes, we do," Damon said.

"Yes," Kira echoed.

"Then you two are bound to one another. In this life and the next." He began tying the binding cord around their wrists, making them one, if only symbolically.

Looking into Damon's eyes, she saw everything she wanted.

"I love you," he whispered to her.

"And I love you."

* * * * *

"Love me, Damon," she moaned, pulling him down onto the bed, her soft body a cushion for his hard one.

He rose above her long enough to free himself of his clothing and then rejoined her, delighting in the way her smooth, soft flesh felt against him. His hands roamed her body as if they were memorizing every curve, every line. She would be his forever, this he vowed.

"Are you wet for me, Kira?" Dipping his fingers into her sweet warmth, he knew the answer. "Do you feel how wet you are?" He ran his fingers along her bottom lip, depositing her nectar there for her to taste. "Taste yourself, love."

Her tongue darted out as she arched her back, forcing her sex to come into contact with his. He inhaled sharply, knowing that if he entered her now it would not last long. All day, he had thought of burying himself deep inside her and never seeing the light of day again. All he wanted was to love her, to be one with her.

"Damon, I love you."

"I love you," he whispered against her neck as he positioned his cock against her opening.

Slowly, he slid into her, filling her completely, not stopping until he felt his cock press against her cervix. He stayed there, his eyes holding hers, his cock buried inside her, refusing to move. This was the sweetest torture, having her folds close around him, her muscles spasm against him, coaxing him to move while he fought against the primal urge. Every muscle in his body tensed with the need to thrust into her. He stilled his breathing, tried to calm the hammering of his heart. Still, the desire to take and take until she had no more to give was fierce.

"Love me, Damon."

"I am loving you."

"No. I mean, move." She arched her back, tilting her hips back, pushing him even further into her, her wetness coating him as he moved.

"If I move, it will not last long. Already, I wish to pour my seed into you." When his voice came out, it sounded like a low growl, evidence of his desire, of his lack of control when it came to her.

She flashed him a wicked smile. "Don't move then."

His breath caught in his throat when her fingers moved down to rub against her clit. They grazed the tender flesh above his penis before they caught her swollen bud. When she began to move her fingers in a circular motion, coaxing an orgasm, pleasuring herself, he remained perfectly still. Her insides quivered, opened and then closed around him. Gently at first. Then, as her movements became more frenzied, they tightened around him like a fist.

He let out a growl as he tried to remain focused, tried not to move. Her fingers moved with increased intensity and her orgasms came one after the other. She moaned, let out a tiny cry, bit her lip. But the whole time, her eyes held his, forcing him to watch the delight as it overtook her face, her body. Unable to wait, unable to remain still, he lifted her hips, held her legs against his chest, and began to thrust into her with such force the entire bed shook.

"Oh, Damon!" she cried beneath him as she flung her head wildly from side to side. Her fingers dug into the bed covering before sinking into his forearms. But he could think of nothing save the sweet feel of ecstasy as her body spasmed around him, squeezing him toward orgasm, promising delights unknown to man.

When his hot seed finally shot into her body, he let out a growl. His heart hammered in his chest, threatened to make him go deaf from the intense sound. And Kira, sweet Kira, opened her arms for him as he sank down onto her, his breathing ragged.

"I shall never let you go," he vowed, taking her breasts into his hands and covering them with kisses. "Never."

Her hand sank into his hair, gently caressing it, stroking it as if he were a babe. This was exactly where he was meant to be and he would convince her of this or die trying.

He groaned low and long. "Come here, woman. Let me show you how much it will help." She gasped as he pulled her against him and then rolled her over. His fingers ran along the mark he had placed on her neck. "You still bear my mark."

"I figured I might."

"I want you to bear more than that. I want you to have my children. Will you do that for me, Kira?"

His cock pressed into her opening, not quite going inside, lingering just on the edges. "Yes, Damon. I will do that for you."

"I love you." His voice sent a shiver through her as it washed over her back.

"I love you."

"Then come for me."

When he drove his cock into her, tremors ripped through her body. There was nothing she would rather do than come for the man who had taken her heart and showed her exactly how love could be.

* * * * *

His arms encircled her, making him feel so incredibly happy, yet so confused by the swirl of emotions that overtook him as his tongue plunged inside her and his breath mixed with hers. Her hands went into his hair, pulling him into her, as he reveled in her taste, hoping this joining would mark the beginning of their life together.

He covered her, his big, strong body pushing her against the bed, the clothing that he had just donned opening underneath her quick fingers. His hands sought her soft chest, reveling in the warmth of her skin and the curves of her body. As his mouth moved down her body, pushing aside her clothing, revealing her nakedness, he pulled away from her hold. She plunged her hands into his hair, tangling around it as he dipped his head lower across her stomach.

"Shall I show you what a dragon can do with his tongue?"

She arched against him, encouraging him to move further, to run his tongue along her mound, to dip inside her, and he knew he would never be the same.

"Not yet, love."

He parted her thighs and settled in over her, his mouth just a breath away. Spreading her open so that her clit stood out, hardened and waiting for his touch, he held her there and gently blew across her skin. A shudder raced through her, forcing her back to arch as she raised herself up for him.

"Please…"

"Please what? Do you want me to please you?"

"Yes."

"No. Not yet. I want to show you something first."

"No. Please." She tried to move but he held her firmly to the bed.

"Lie still."

"I am going to show you how I can make you come without touching you."

This time when his breath blew across her, she squirmed beneath him, but he still didn't lighten his hold on her. He breathed again and then again. With each breath, the heat increased while her clit visibly throbbed, begging for release, begging to be touched, teased, rubbed.

"Come for me and then I'll take you."

"I can't."

"Yes, you can. And you will."

His breath rushed over her once more and this time he felt the orgasm build deep inside. When she came it was as if a rush of color danced in her eyes.

"You taste like heaven," he whispered.

"Please, Damon."

He ignored her pleas, running his tongue along the outer edges of her folds, avoiding her clit, avoiding her opening. Her juices spilled out as he moved over her. When his tongue finally brushed against her clit she let out a cry and then the tremors took over her body. She thrashed against the bed, pulling at the covers, her body urging him to take her, to release her, to end the madness that was taking over them both.

He finally lifted above her and pressed against her, warning her of his impending invasion. And she was more than ready, opening for him, spreading her thighs wide. His hair fell into her face, brushed against her breasts. She arched against him, encouraging him to slide into her, to give her what she wanted and to fulfill the promise his body made to her.

"Do you want me?"

"Yes. More than I want to breathe."

"Good."

With that one word, he entered her, filling her completely, stretching her further than she remembered being stretched before. His cock pressed against her cervix, remaining still.

"I want you to look at me. Know that I will always love you."

He kissed her tears as he moved inside her. His cock slid in and out gently, loving her rather than taking her in a wildly savage way. This was new, too. The depth of feeling she invoked was enough to make his heart almost burst from the fullness. He took her hands in his, wove his fingers with hers and continued to move slowly inside her, taking his time, feeling out every single inch of her womanhood.

His hair brushed against her face before he brought his mouth down to gently cover hers. When his lips met hers they teased at first, lightly kissing the outer edges of her mouth. Then his tongue darted out to lick first her top lip and then her bottom one. Wrapping his arms around her, he pulled her close and rested her head against his chest. Slowly, he rolled them over so that she lay on top of him.

"I want you to love me." He smiled up at her.

"I do love you."

She rose above him as he placed his arms behind his neck.

"You have amazing breasts." His eyes were focused on her chest as she began to move on him. "I like to watch them move as you move."

She began rocking slowly on him, setting her own pace.

She dipped her fingers down across her wetness, which had pooled between her body and Damon's and then used the wetness to moisten her clit so her finger would slide around it easier. The sensation immediately caused his climax to threaten. He wasn't ready to come yet, wasn't ready to descend from the heights, to return to the mortal realm, but he could no longer deny it.

The orgasm ripped through her body and she clung to him as he pounded into her, nearing his release. A growl erupted from deep in his chest as his seed spilled into her.

* * * * *

As the moons rose over the land, Kira settled into her new husband's arms and pulled him tightly into her embrace.

They had formed a bond with their bodies, just as they had with their words. In three days they would go to his home, to the palace, and confront his brother. No, not confront. Plan the future. Mace and Damon would overcome their differences now that they had both found love. Kira smiled in the darkness as Damon rested in her arms. Somehow, she had traveled across the galaxy twice for this man. His blood beat inside her veins and his heart was somehow connected to hers. She should have known it the moment she set eyes on him.

New Orleans seemed so far away. It was another lifetime ago. And her fear of living without a past was no longer an issue. Damon had given her a past, but he had done so much more for her. He had also given her a future.

The End

Enjoy this excerpt from

Ellora's Cavemen

Tales from the Temple II

Mace
Dragon's Law

Alicia Sparks

Chapter One

Near Waydon, a small village near Tyr on the planet Tyr-LaRoche. Modern Day.

The wind howled, forcing the tiny hairs on Eleanora's neck to stand at attention. She swallowed the lump that had formed in her throat and waited. The night birds that had been singing their welcome to the moon only seconds before were quiet now, as if they anticipated the arrival of some menacing force that would rip them from the sky. The clearing was illuminated by the light moon as the dark one hung, a black circle in the night's sky, signaling what would soon be coming.

The thunderous footsteps seemed to echo as they approached. Eleanora listened as tree branches snapped and leaves crunched beneath the power of the beast that made its way to the sacrificial site. Perspiration formed on her hands as they remained tethered in place. She was prepared for whatever the fates had deemed would be her destiny. As the dragon approached, she raised her chin, willing herself to face her death as her sisters had faced theirs. If only she could be the last sacrifice, a guarantee that the villagers would no longer strive to sate the dragon's blood lust.

The dragon crouched before her and let out a piercing growl, forcing her to flinch, her bravery fleeing. A slow chill crept up her back as her eyes ran over the dragon's frame. He was no bigger than a man, but his domineering presence in the clearing was enough to make that chill break into a full-blown shudder. She had never seen a dragon at such close range and had no idea what to expect of him. This was certainly not it. Still, he was commanding enough to make her rethink her plan of attack, which was to use magick to free herself and render him helpless. She cringed when she caught sight of his tail, which swished like a cat's and was double the length of his body. The tail looked harmless at first glance, but the spines there were known for the poison they injected into his victims. Her hands clutched into fists as she contemplated her best plan of attack. A wave of nausea threatened to overtake her. In spite of her trepidation, she was held spellbound by the strength of his frame.

She raked her eyes over his scaly body and bit her lip as she raised her head, daring to look at his face. The profile was almost human, but there was nothing human about the way he lingered over her body, prepared to make her his latest meal as his hot breath swept across her face.

The howl echoed once more, conjuring tremors throughout her body, but his approach ceased when he lifted his head to sniff the air as if he sensed someone else here. Her hands froze, and her entire body stood stock-still. The dragon caught her eyes only for a second, but she felt the image of raw pain that reflected in those gray pools.

He turned and flicked his tail back and forth before he pounced.

The dragon covered her body as he let out a howl that sounded like pain. Eleanora tried to steady her breathing, tried to recover from her moment in the dragon's eyes, but her body refused to cooperate. She should act now and save herself, but her arms wouldn't move. The piercing sound of the dragon's roar forced her into action. The jolt of electricity that shot through her body at the sound of his cry was enough to move her once-frozen limbs.

The words were said in an instant, almost before she could think her way through the spell. As soon as they fled her lips, the shackles fell to the ground, releasing her from her temporary prison. Only now, two dragons hindered her move toward safety.

Her passage was blocked as the black one, the one whose eyes she had seen so clearly. Then the red one advanced, charging forward, challenging the black one for dominance. Eleanora was trapped, unable to move between or around the dragons, unable to save herself. Cowering to the ground, Eleanora lay spellbound as the black dragon covered her body, protecting her from the fury of the red.

In the next seconds, the black let out a howl and blood flowed from the long razor cuts along its back. It circled around the red, the two looking like wild animals challenging one another for a meal. She swallowed hard. If they sensed she was still here in the darkness, neither gave notice.

She drew in her breath, once more determined to end the wreckage brought upon her village by the dragons. Every ounce of courage she may have had hours ago died inside her as she contemplated her approach. Two ferocious beasts fought just a few yards away from her. And never before had she felt as inconsequential as she did at this moment.

Then, at the last moment, the red dragon misjudged. He caught sight of her, distracting him enough to give the black an advantage. Bleeding, howling in pain, the black leapt, sinking his teeth into the jugular.

The red didn't fall as she expected. She knew dragons must lose much more blood than a shallow cut could render. And they healed more quickly than humans. But the black hadn't given up his quest. Eleanora's eyes widened as he leapt once more, this time practically ripping the vein from his opponent's neck.

The black turned now, having worn the red to weakness. The red lay in a heap under the moonlight, his blood already ceasing to flow. Before she had time to react, everything went black.

Enjoy this excerpt from
Better Than Ice Cream
© Copyright Alicia Sparks 2004

Ryan would have spilled his water had he been holding it. Instead, he breathed in small gasps, trying to calm himself as she flipped open the container and licked her finger before sticking it into the white substance. He sat on the edge of his seat as he watched her insert the finger between her full, red lips. Jaw clenched, he wondered how it would feel to insert something else there, wondered if it would light the fire in her eyes the way his sugar just had. His body reacted to the thought, and his jeans tightened. So much for unattractive. This meant one thing. Laura Reynolds was going to be one of those difficult girls he avoided at all costs. Funny, avoiding her didn't seem to be in his vocabulary right now.

"Oh, yeah," she sighed. "This is just what I needed."

Ryan had a flashback from *When Harry Met Sally* and hoped the sugar hadn't been *that* good. He'd hate to be outdone by a sweetener.

"This is incredible. You got any other surprises there?" she teased.

He leaned forward, meeting her challenge. When her eyes widened, he realized he'd caught her off guard. "Why don't you come over here and see?"

Breathing in relief when panic flashed across her face, he knew she was teasing him. Still, she fascinated him. Had Laura Reynolds been this cute in high school? Cute. He suppressed an inward laugh. There wasn't a damn thing cute about her. She was sin incarnate. No wonder she could create an ice cream that caused orgasms. She could cause them from across the room. He wished he carried a pencil with him to drop under the table so he could get a glance at those legs. The cleavage he caught before she hid it behind the menu. He hoped the lump in his throat went away soon.

"Your tea," the waiter interrupted.

"Allow me." Ryan took the sugar and spooned it into her tea and then his, imagining how he would much rather dip her finger into his glass.

"Thanks." She smiled and then took a big sip. "Wow. It's even better like this." She drank another big sip of the tea. "This is really good."

"So do we have a deal?"

"I don't know. We haven't really discussed the deal yet. What are your terms?"

"Well, first, I need to know more about your product. To be sure mine will remain stable." He tried to ignore the stirring in his pants. Damn, he'd been without a woman for too long, and Laura looked just like the kind of sin he needed to end the dry spell.

"I'm sure I can make yours remain firm," she sipped at the tea again, apparently ignoring her own sexual comment.

Firm. He shifted in his seat. Damn it. This was supposed to be a harmless business dinner. Not an outrageous flirtation with Laura Reynolds. "I'm sure you can. I don't suppose you have any of that orgasm producing ice cream up your dress, do you?"

The smile disappeared from her lips. He won the banter, sending her a look that let her know he wouldn't be afraid to go looking for said ice cream.

"No. But I do have some back at my place." She bit her lip, making him wonder if she regretted the invitation. "Excuse me for a minute." She stood, grabbing her bag, and pushed past him as he stood.

Ten minutes and she had run for the hills. *Welcome home, Ryan*. He watched her disappear behind the wall dividing the bar from the restaurant. He sank back into his chair, mulling over her invitation and reaction to it.

He was a LeJeune. A sex machine. That's what the women in his life had always expected from him. And he had produced. Millions of satisfied customers. Well, not exactly millions. And it *had* been a long time.

He hadn't been with a woman in over a year. The town's gossip mill wouldn't buy that. A LeJeune without a woman was like summer in Louisiana without thunderstorms. It was a rare occurrence.

Hell, he was thirty-three years old. Past time to settle down. He picked up the decanter of sugar and closed it, concentrating on the click to indicate the top was back in place.

Laura Reynolds.

He could play, couldn't he? Tease. See what she was all about. It would be harmless. Right?

About the author:

Alicia's interest in romance began as a child when she used to hide out reading her mom's forbidden romance novels. She remembers very distinctly the first time she ever read *Gone with the Wind* and was instantly hooked on the concept of the Southern gentlemanly rake. She likes to think that there's a little bit of Rhett in all of her heroes, whether they be sexy cowboys or dark and brooding rock stars.

Always writing against a soundtrack, Alicia finds inspiration for her cowboys and contemporary heroes from country musicians such as Kenny Chesney. Her love for the gothadelic sounds of Type O Negative has inspired several vampire stories and stories about tragically beautiful musicians. Other inspirations include the music of Saliva, Van Halen, Santana, Blake Shelton, and Prince. (She's a Gemini. That explains the wide variety of influences!)

Alicia has completed several manuscripts ranging from comedic contemporaries to dark, sexy paranormals and fantastical futuristics.

Her favorite ice cream is Godiva's dark chocolate truffle. Eaten straight from the container, it is almost—almost—as good as reading erotica!

Alicia welcomes mail from readers. You can write to her c/o Ellora's Cave Publishing at 1056 Home Avenue, Akron OH 44310-3502.

Why an electronic book?

We live in the Information Age—an exciting time in the history of human civilization in which technology rules supreme and continues to progress in leaps and bounds every minute of every hour of every day. For a multitude of reasons, more and more avid literary fans are opting to purchase e-books instead of paperbacks. The question to those not yet initiated to the world of electronic reading is simply: *why?*

1. *Price.* An electronic title at Ellora's Cave Publishing and Cerridwen Press runs anywhere from 40-75% less than the cover price of the <u>exact same title</u> in paperback format. Why? Cold mathematics. It is less expensive to publish an e-book than it is to publish a paperback, so the savings are passed along to the consumer.

2. *Space.* Running out of room to house your paperback books? That is one worry you will never have with electronic novels. For a low one-time cost, you can purchase a handheld computer designed specifically for e-reading purposes. Many e-readers are larger than the average handheld, giving you plenty of screen room. Better yet, hundreds of titles can be stored within your new library—a single microchip. (Please note that Ellora's Cave and Cerridwen Press does not endorse any specific brands. You can check our website at www.ellorascave.com or

www.cerridwenpress.com for customer recommendations we make available to new consumers.)

3. *Mobility.* Because your new library now consists of only a microchip, your entire cache of books can be taken with you wherever you go.

4. *Personal preferences are accounted for.* Are the words you are currently reading too small? Too large? Too...**ANNOYING**? Paperback books cannot be modified according to personal preferences, but e-books can.

5. *Instant gratification.* Is it the middle of the night and all the bookstores are closed? Are you tired of waiting days—sometimes weeks—for online and offline bookstores to ship the novels you bought? Ellora's Cave Publishing sells instantaneous downloads 24 hours a day, 7 days a week, 365 days a year. Our e-book delivery system is 100% automated, meaning your order is filled as soon as you pay for it.

Those are a few of the top reasons why electronic novels are displacing paperbacks for many an avid reader. As always, Ellora's Cave and Cerridwen Press welcomes your questions and comments. We invite you to email us at service@ellorascave.com, service@cerridwenpress.com or write to us directly at: 1056 Home Ave. Akron OH 44310-3502.

COMING TO A BOOKSTORE NEAR YOU!

ELLORA'S CAVE
2005
BEST SELLING AUTHORS TOUR

NEED A MORE EXCITING
WAY TO PLAN YOUR DAY?

ELLORA'S
CAVEMEN
2006 CALENDAR

COMING THIS FALL